Cab Tales

Presented to

Barbara Bush Branch Library

By

Barbara Bush Library Friends

Cab Tales

Eric Muirhead

Temple and Dallas, Texas

ISBN: 978-0-9839715-4-2
Library of Congress Control Number: 2012936909

Revised Second Edition, Ink Brush Press, 2012; First Edition, Panther
Creek Press, 2003; Manufactured in the United States of America

Ink Brush Press
Temple and Dallas, Texas

for
Robert Phillips

Acknowledgments

Several journals first published stories included in *Cab Tales:*

Texas Short Fiction: A World In Itself, "Carmen"
Texas Short Fiction, Vol. II, "Drag"
New Texas 93, "Sphinx"
New Texas 95, "Metal"
Concho River Review, "Stetson"
i.e. magazine, "Dolores"
RiverSedge, "The Weed Patch"
Reflections 92, "Justice" and "Dark Side of the Moon"
Reflections 94, "Mockingbird"
Texas Magazine, "Africa"

CONTENTS

Author's Foreword

The night streets of a large city begin a motion of souls different from those that know the day. These night souls wear no mask: loners, outcasts, the strange, the different, the lost, angels battered by life, angels heavy with life, the angry, the damned, those other angels just plying their trade. And making this motion possible is the cabby, who, as ferryman, sets these night souls in passage and confession. He listens, hears, and even should he struggle to comprehend, he knows in their stories a depth and mystery far from the light that is yet the telling tale of all of us. The night streets of a large city are the mask removed, revealing a face, a void that can only be thought of as the raw heart of life. The night cabby hears it beat. From trip to trip, shift to shift, he hears it: daunting sometimes, appalling even, seductive other times, wooing, but always powerful, a force, this raw heart beating that is the story of these his passengers, their mission, their pain, their raison d'être only night is able to make known.

The cabby ferries them, and before it's over he's become every one of them, become his own raw heart of life that beats, himself a void because his mask too is now ripped away. And what he is, once the sun rises and floods the night streets with light, is just this void that is all there is to see. And all he ever can be, what future there is, is now only possible because the sun has shown the truth only night is able to make known.

Eric Muirhead
April 2012

Stetson

He slid into the front seat with a presence already filling the cab and powering against me well before he had settled himself in and drawn the door to with a most decisively gentle click. The white Stetson was like a cake across the top of the interior, crowning the impressive height of him—from the shine of a pair of black cowboy boots, up the dark length of a trim three-piece business suit, to the tanned face of a man in his healthy fifties basking at me out of blue, boy eyes asplash in just the lightest spray of sun wrinkles. The easy smile seemed to draw all the relaxation of his long body to itself, as he nodded with a debonair air of assured rightness in all things, even 4-door sedans that were too cramped to accommodate him.

"The Dome," he said simply. His voice was dark saddle leather, what you like just feeling in your hands over and over.

"You mean the Astrodome?" I said, in a bit of a flutter.

"That's what I said," he replied. And drawing his long left arm up over the top of the seat, his hand almost at my shoulder, he turned to gaze forward with the barest audible crinkling of all his gatheredness, and awaited my response at the accelerator.

I pulled away from the dark glassed facade of the Hyatt

to my left, the rocketing streaks of bulbs that marked the glassfront elevators up the back of the lobby already a dazzling brightness—like white fireworks running straight up into the sky—in the premature twilight here deep from the sun. But that hat on his tall figure had appeared equally as white as he emerged from the hotel, strolling up to flag me down with a mere gesture of his index finger as if I had been appointed all along to be there for him. And since he'd surprisingly taken the front seat of my new '73 Plymouth, not the back, I was so pumped up all I could think was to go, go, get him to what was fortunately an obvious destination, the Dome, that didn't require I disgrace myself by needing the Key Map to find it—even I couldn't miss that flying saucer of a roof hovering whitely over the southern outskirts of the city.

But it was rush hour, the work force of downtown now freed from a million desks to make its way out. I wanted to cross all the northbound lanes of Louisiana for a quick right turn over to Main, but in the density of traffic managed only a single lane before stopped by the light. Now needing two additional blocks headed the wrong way in this one-way maze, I sighed, rather rudely and loud really, as I stared over the wheel. Even with the windows down and cool February air drifting through the cab, I couldn't help it, I was feeling hemmed in, almost squeezed, between the tightness and bulk of the cars all around, and the enormity and poise of this magnate Stetson beside me, who seemed an incarnation I thought only myth anymore of that cattle-rancher ethos Texas had long ago established as its heart.

The light changed.

"Aren't you going to charge me?" he suddenly asked.

The meter flag! Damn, I thought, and tried to ease it over as if I always gave my passengers the benefit of a few free moments. "Yes, of course," I said, turning instantly meek as I glanced back for a lane change and caught him looking at me. His face was inquisitive, amused, and I prickled under an outbreak of sweat that he stared at me that way. But when we stopped again I saw that he had turned to look ahead and conduct his own thoughts.

"You know," I uttered in a stab at aplomb to break the silence, as we awaited a right turn at McKinney in the bottleneck of traffic between Shell One and the Tenneco Building, "the Oilers are finished with their season, and the Astros are just starting spring training, aren't they? In Florida. So what's going on at the Dome?"

His eyebrows shot straight up beneath that Stetson, and with a quirky, amazed move of head and hat he looked at me. He even pulled his hand back from between us. "Don't you know? Why, the Livestock Show and Rodeo." The light changed and I dived for a chance to hide this fresh embarrassment behind some deft attention to the wheel: amounting to all of a cramped right turn only, and a dead halt behind bumper after bumper of cars stacked in front of us. "It is only *the* rodeo, son. *The* event of the year. Don't you know?"

I kept my eyes to the windshield, unable to bear his stupefaction. But that moment unable to bear what was worse, my stupefaction, that I was here behind the wheel of a yellow cab. Four years out of college, the laurels of an Ivy League education, and, until recently, wearing the white coat and learning the needs of the sick toward the medical degree that had brought me to Houston in the first place.

But I had thrown it away.

Even trashed my Yale diploma in a night of cold, stoned rage. Feeling trapped, defined, the white coat and years of training become a straightjacket, and I wild to get out. Wanting to fly, somehow fly.

I stared at the irreality of it all, my future at age twenty-five just a blank out that windshield before me.

While my passenger stared at me. I could feel his eyes gauging this stranger I'd become to myself.

"You're new, aren't you?" I heard him say.

I turned and looked at him. He was drawn back, his blue eyes narrowed in anticipation of my response, but a kind of half smile beginning to hover on his face. "Yes, I'm afraid so," I acknowledged. "This is my first trip ever, in fact. I just came in from the cab lot, over the Elysian Viaduct into downtown, as green as grass at this job, and was wandering around, not sure where to start, when you flagged me down. You've chosen a number one driver, sir, in more ways than you could possibly know."

It began with a single guffaw, choked back for a moment, but unable to hold itself, coming on, at last reaching crescendo, a rocking spirited laugh that fairly bellowed from his sun-washed face, gusting high out his window into the high air of every skyscraper around us. He threw his head back so far as he laughed, in fact, that I thought he might mash that great hat against the ceiling. But magically it resisted any dinge to itself; even in this tightness it seemed to float and command. The light changed.

"Oh, I thought so, I thought so. Brand new." I was easing

us forward as he continued to exult in an aftermath of chuckles welling up through him. "Yes, I thought so."

But maybe my failure to say anything sent a bother through his mirth, for he suddenly reined himself in and eyed me as we halted for another red light. "Well, that's okay, son," he announced. "After all, it's things new keep this world on track. Now isn't that the truth."

"Is it on track? Sorry, but it hardly seems so to me."

"Now what do you think any of us are good for?" he said, as if mildly offended. "Of course it's on track. And nowhere more than here, in this fine city. Hell, son, it's people like you who make Houston what it is. Why, there's no newer place on earth. Space City, and it's taking us to the stars. Isn't that where we're all going?"

I looked at him, the animation of his last words resident in the full pride with which he looked at me in return. I saw that he believed everything he said. Or at least was determined to, as if mere affirmation, like donning that hat, was all that was necessary to turn a faith into truth.

"And what a way to be doing your part," he continued gaily. "New to the point of not even remembering you're supposed to be making money. I mean, how far do you think we might have gone before you thought of that meter?"

"You mean, *if* I thought of that meter." I couldn't help seeing myself gliding coolly up to the Astrodome, ready for my first fare ever, the fruits of my labor, and. . . nothing but little blank windows excusing themselves from the meter box. I could even see him laughing, exulting again, as he strode off to his rodeo after some kindly remuneration for my incompetence. "Believe me, sir, in my case it's a big 'if'."

5

"But that's exactly it, son. 'If'. Nothing keeps things more in order than 'if'. It's the cutting edge of everything that's new. It's like the shadow leading us through the light, cutting the way. I mean, what else is life but a big 'if'? It's pathfinding, is all."

"A shadow that leads us?" I replied. "My alma mater's motto was 'light and truth', if you'll forgive me for saying so. It was *Lux et Veritas* everywhere I looked. And that's what brought me to Houston, B.A. and all: 'light and truth.' But 'a shadow that leads us'? That begins to make sense to me now, I have to tell you."

He calculated my remarks, their bitterness, his eyes narrowed on me a moment. "Well, of course it's just an expression. After all, son, you don't have shadow without light, now do you? So maybe we're just talking words. But hell, little is predictable, that's just it. I mean, you certainly weren't predictable, were you?" And I saw that half smile hovering on his face again, the pleased blue of his eyes. "Here you are with a B.A., fancy motto and all, and you're driving a cab? That's got first written all over it." And he laughed again for a moment, though lightly, and turned to gaze out his open side window.

I worked a right onto Main Street, easing through the crowd of pedestrians that filled the crosswalk. We were headed south at last, through the heart of downtown Houston.

"But wasn't that the pioneer spirit after all?" my passenger suddenly said, turning back at me in a rebound from his thoughts, as I began to sense trouble on this street, some kind of obstruction down the way. "Little was predictable, anything could happen, yet people made their way. The light was always there, in the end, for those who persevered."

"Well, I wish I could think of myself as a pioneer," I said, selfishly returning the relevance of all this to me, and feeling already a rising irritation that traffic was stalling in front of us, "but I don't think so. Pioneering's dead, anyway, isn't it? There's certainly none of it anywhere I look."

"No, no, son." He seemed aghast at what I said, troubled to the very peak of that great hat bearing down on me with the full weight of his concern. "No. If you don't see it then you're not looking. Everyone's a pioneer, at least of sorts, making their way against the unpredictable. That hasn't stopped just because we reached the Pacific Ocean and built cities across the plain. It's going on every day, every moment. Everyone's cutting their way forward; it's certainly not given to them. Hell, it's basic, son. Just look all around you. You know, Dick and Jane stuff. Look, look, look."

See Spot run. Yes, I remembered that. Overwhelmed by such insistence, and his left arm even gesturing out at the city to urge me to it, I did look: at brisk secretaries clattering the sidewalks of Main in tight scurry of their skirts and heels, hugging purses and striding for car or bus or man some-where; at executives and lawyers, less defined or fast, in suits floppy with fatigue, swinging their briefcases and gazing blankly ahead of them at whatever near dreams bemused their faces; and the loitering crowd of shoe-shiners and indigents mixing in in indolent contradiction to it all. And everywhere else, crowding every available space, the cars, in a tight phalanx all around us, now trying to move obediently and slowly forward in response to a green light: a solid testudo of exodus and the American dream realized.

Pioneers? More like Dick and Jane, I thought.

And amazing that when I was reading that primer as a snotty first-grader my passenger was in his thirties already, maybe even sporting that same hat, as he swung the deals of his cattle, his empire. I looked at him, hoping his preacherly rhetoric only a well-disguised, recreant wit having fun at my expense. Another version of his laughter maybe.

But nothing like that revealed itself. He was simply absorbed out his side window, so the back of his hat filled my view. I looked at that sweep of white hiding his head. He could have been a little boy under that hat and it would have reached as tall.

Or was that what he was?

We weren't moving anymore. Cars in the southbound lanes filled the intersection at Polk, unable to budge, even with the light green. It turned yellow, red. Now cross traffic was blocked. I regretted I hadn't taken McKinney over to Fannin and its one-way thoroughfare south. But no left turns were allowed off Main for many blocks yet, and we were stuck. The sense of being hemmed in grew strong again. I began to chafe. No one honked, it was strangely frozen, stopped.

Gone automatically to timer, the meter clicked another $.20, without forward motion at all. I worried my passenger would think I'd chosen this slow, gummed-up route on purpose, to run up the fare.

But the Stetson, to my astonishment, just sat leisurely, his hands on his knees, and rocked, ever so slightly, rapt in everything around us with that half smile floating once more on his countenance—his hat, in fact, almost a metronome, in swing to some strange, inner click of his pleasure at the jostling hurry of the pedestrians out his side window and the stalled confusion of the vehicles everywhere else. He seemed to swell, filling with some kind of energy and abundance at what he saw. "Oh, I like this city," he suddenly exulted in his baritone. "You know, I like this city. I just got in this morning from New York, and I've been missing ole Houston." And with that he took a deep breath of satisfaction, then leaned back, releasing a long, gracious sigh, like a man replete after a meal, and, stretching his legs as much as he could, draped his long left arm once again over the seat between us, settling into reverie. Suddenly he began thrumming the fingers of his left hand in the close proximity of my right ear.

It was an instant irritation. And he cocked his head my way as he mused, his hat leaning further, further into me.

Tiny increments of advance. We made it across Clay. I finally saw that the lights up ahead, at Jefferson, were blinking. A damn hour for a utility crew to be working! And all the while his fingers thrummed at a gallop in my ear, utterly content, utterly unself-conscious, fraying my patience.

The sun had hit the horizon somewhere far beyond the superstructure of the Gulf Freeway, which had come into view curving around the near perimeter of downtown, the stretch known locally as the Pierce Elevated, as bogged and stilled with traffic as we, as quiet. Headlights were coming on, and in the strange peace of all this density shadows were on the rise everywhere to commingle like silent bat wings in the first hints of night.

But I couldn't indulge the greater pattern. His fingers

9

thrummed, and my nerves were becoming hard to contain.

We were at Jefferson, the red lights blinking bright in the dusk. "Do you notice how Houstonians don't honk?" the Stetson suddenly said. "At least, not much. I mean, I've just come from New York, I told you, and with something like this those people just honk and honk. Everybody blaring. But not here. As if no one wants to spoil the beauty of sundown.

Disbelief just popped, like a blister, from the rib cage of my confinement. His amazing reverence for the marriage of big country and big city that was the paradox and paralysis of Houston this crowded hour, his first grade soul reading Dick and Jane and the extraordinary in everything just ordinary, was just too much for me. And just like that, snatched into the cool, late winter evening, my earlier sense of vulnerability and wonder before this fantasy case of a cattleman now bolted at the quixotic reality that now seemed the only conceivable truth about him.

"Well, I took up cab driving to fly, if you want to know the truth," I blurted out in vexation. Immediately I gunned the accelerator across the Jefferson intersection.

"To fly, hey," he remarked. We both jerked forward as I slammed the brake. My tires squealed embarrassingly as I nearly rear-ended the car in front of me at the Calhoun light. Exasperated I looked at my passenger. But he didn't register the near-accident at all, instead locked on me in a clean, amazed stare of those boy eyes, and that strange half smile flirting with his face again. He even stopped the tiresome thrumming of his fingers. "To fly?" he repeated, his smile widening. Sensing another laugh about to come my way, I tried to dodge his eyes, but found I couldn't. They were riding down on me as on horses, and I recoiled at what seemed their pumped-up quaintness of self-satisfaction.

"I grew up in Dallas," I said abruptly, "and I've lived elsewhere. But I never found the Texas that you seem to be. Tell me, do you own a King Ranch somewhere?"

He looked stunned, even hurt, by this. Maybe to recover he chuckled in a nervous, unconvincing way, and pulled his arm from between us to readjust his hat with a slight tug at the brim. He glanced out the side, then forward, as if looking out there for an answer. His face at that instant looked suddenly tired. "Oh, I own a little bit of everything, all around."

That was all, apparently, I was going to get. We were crossing Calhoun when I saw his eyes come back at me with a plea for trust. But I was feeling advantage, as if I had found a lever to force him into the open, prove him the charlatan I was now convinced he was. "Well, if it's things new keep this world on track, as you say, then what about you? Are you new?" I didn't hide the tinge of scorn—abrogating every principle of the cabby to be nothing but a driver and a receptive listener, I didn't care. I was even thinking I might quit after this first trip, anyway, so it didn't matter.

"I rue the day I stop, son. But then, I'll be dead, won't I?"

The simple dignity of that leather voice passed like a wind through me, a benediction on the whole, crowded, bogged down moment in which I found him my partner, and down into which I was trying to drag him against his nature. "It's a matter of liking things, son," he added. "Why the world shouldn't seem new, every day, I don't know. If you can't like, you may as well pack your bags and take a midnight train for

11

nowhere. Just disappear down your own track and leave the world to itself. But it's your loss, is all I have to say.

"After all," he went on, "you're new, aren't you? Don't know what brought you to cab driving, and with a B.A. no less. But something did. And here you are."

"I quit medical school," I said. "Only last month. I hated it." I sagged. It was suddenly inexplicable what I had done, unforgivable. "Almost had my M.D. in fact."

"Well then, son. You had your reasons, didn't you?" But I couldn't answer that. If I had them, they had blown like so much dust from this empty bin I now recognized my life to be. "Life is all about reasons, I guess," the Stetson continued. "Although they're not really the important thing still, are they? What I own is. . . just what I do, not really reasons actually. The reasons are there, but where nobody wants to look to get at 'em. What if I told you I own nothing really. I mean nothing."

I looked at him. But his face was struggling somewhere between that half smile and an odd distortion that almost seemed he was playing games and didn't mind if I knew it. Teasing me with the charlatan I had wanted to prove he was. I looked right into eyes that appeared transparency of something dark and laughing, diabolic for the instant. The great hat was all shadow over it.

"Well," I said uncomfortably, wondering what I had done to chase the boy and his brightness away from that face, "I would find that hard to believe."

"Fine, son. Then that's how it should be."

He said it with almost disdainful finality, then turned away. I saw only the back of his hat as he looked out his side window. Unnerved by the abruptness of his response, and the way he seemed to be shutting me off, I proceeded into a smoother flow of traffic now we were out of downtown and clear of the Pierce Elevated. As our pace picked up, however, my passenger only slipped further from me, into a silence that seemed his own island. He cocked his right elbow out his open window and just looked away at the passing blocks of small businesses and stores, and old dark-brick apartment houses, that accompanied Main for this stretch of city. It was a sector of Houston I had always found boring, and but little improved in this time of twilight, yet it seemed to be drawing him away from me, deep into thoughts that were impenetrable.

The blocks dimmed into glare of headlights and taillights in contrary flow, darkness shading rapidly the nondescript passing of the city through here, and shading him who sat beside me. Only the white hat seemed immune, as it rode his figure like a lighted ship in the dark of the cab, a talisman of this man's mystery I suddenly grew impatient again to force into the open. I couldn't figure whether he was thoroughly incognito, or just the reverse. Was he trying to hide a history, or did he have a history to hide?

"Tell me, sir," I ventured, to break the silence, "is that hat real. . . or is it just for show?"

He jerked around abruptly. "I mean," I stumbled on, headlong on, "that hat of yours. . . I mean. . . isn't that sort of thing, well. . . just for show anymore? Like the Livestock Show you're going to?"

It was like he was hit by a gust of wind that blew his whole face wide and that Stetson tumbling back off his head

and away and away into rushing dust of his astonishment.
The way he looked at me. As a man all of whose clothes blew
off him and revealed him naked in front of crowds who
hadn't yet overcome their consternation enough to point.

"What?" He gagged.

"I was only asking. I mean. . ."

"For *show*?"

"I mean. . ."

"*Sheeeit*, son."

"Well. . . that hat. . . what else?"

"*Show*? And a King Ranch somewhere too, right?"

"Well . . . I just meant. . ."

"Son, I've been to the moon. I was with Armstrong and
I wore this hat. You believe that, don't you?"

"Well, it did seem you must own—"

"Own? Why, son, I own *everything. Everything.*"

It was some kind of renaissance in our confined front
seat of a cab. For he started to laugh, from up the deep-down
length of him like purest water roiling up from pressures
buried, shattering strata in staccato bursts from his frame,
finally a geyser in full plume. He whooped and splashed his
pleasure in an inundation over me: for I was laughing too,
reaping my own apostasy and doubt in a flood of acquies-
cence. And into a changing character of city we mellowed but
little—by "The Sanctuary", a church turned disco and lurid
light show, the flashing reds and blues and yellows already
dancing off the inside of stained glass as we passed, and
muted from within, as if reverberating from the bowels of the
earth, the voice and guitar of Jimi Hendrix wailing the lyrics
of "All Along the Watchtower" (*Two riders were*

14

approaching / And the wind began to howl): "Now there's a church for sore eyes," he said. "Hell finally claiming the sanctuary. If people would just figure it, that hell's as predictable, as necessary, as the coming of sunrise and sundown. Just 'light and truth', hey son? The grass comin' up green, the wheat," and he winked at me. "The church's been trying to stop the earth in its course ever since preachers, the only justification it's been able to find for itself. But that, no question, is a church I like."—by the gilt whiteness of the Warwick radiant with mirrors and chandeliered brightness reflected in planes: "I learned when staying there once," he said, "that you are what you seem, and by God if all those mirrors and concierges and posh folk don't show it back at you. Seem the best and you are the best."—and around the flood-lit plashings of the Mecom Fountain streaming light in curls: "I was arrested there once for swimming without a permit. Best thing I ever did in a black tie." "Did you have on that hat?" "Why, of course. Only reason the police saw me; otherwise I'm a pretty good merman. But this hat's a hell of a buoy, you know. Keeps you up high where everybody can see you. Life's about floating, after all. Remember that." —then beneath the canopy of live oaks lining South Main darkly from this point on in brooding ranks of Parisian neatness. His hat now in the gnarled, tree-heavy darkness like a light-floating full moon off my shoulder, but his ebullience subsiding as abruptly back into his interior as it had arisen.

He was looking, as if strangely quieted, into the darkness of it all outside his window, into the trees of Rice University where blackbirds in their millions were screeching on their nightly return to roost as we passed by. "That's my alma mater," he said, but rather sadly. I wanted him to continue, to say something more about this place Rice, where birds screech deafeningly at twilight, and the guano—I had seen it on walks through there—plastered the ground beneath the live oaks in a rich uric smell that permeated the air. But the playful vein of the last moments was gone from him. He was just staring out there, now far away, as we thrust our way south.

His Stetson seemed to sink on him. He seemed to grow small. He was suddenly the lonely frontier of an old man over by the door, shrunk by the pull of some deep regret, apparently, calling him into himself. But whatever it was exactly, the Stetson, as he kept his head turned from me, proved a blanket to his mystery.

And his mystery was all there was in the end. I had gotten no further by then than I had been at the beginning: only the miles that measured themselves from the Hyatt to the Dome. And through the return of bright lights south of Rice, by that mini-city of power, the Texas Medical Center, so recently home to my wanderings in the white coat—all the banks and medicine and hotels cleaving the young night in a glitter of prosperity as insular to me now as a space station—he remained silent and aloof, swallowed in the void of himself, and his hat only a sweeping testimony to aloneness decked out in a tasteful extravagance of whimsy and transience.

"Your loss," he had said. I wondered whose midnight train he had been speaking of.

Easing through the crowded acres of parking lot from the

Kirby Drive entrance, up to the great stadium itself, ablaze like a round glass palace in the deepening twilight of the Gulf sky, I was feeling suddenly desperate and empty that I would lose this guy; at least whatever really claimed him in that soul of his seemed in crazy need of being said. If somehow, of course, it had not been his laughter, or the birds screeching in the darkness of Rice U., that had already said it. But he was invisible to me. Added to it all, a certain disgust rose up that I was depositing him here—all the pushing and movement of humanity and cars here, beneath that gleaming white hemisphere drawing the thousands unto itself, only seemed a make-believe of enormous proportions against the single man beneath his Stetson. And yet, what can I say, as I pulled up close to West Gate and stopped, the boy eyes were back in that suave face, resurrected as if the Astrodome itself had breathed them into him. He bounced out of the cab, slammed the door, and leaned low his length to the window as he pulled his wallet from his back pocket. He passed across to me a bill folded crisply in his fingers.

It was a fifty. For a twelve dollar fare. "Now, son," he said, "go out there and make a few dollars. And, son. . ." But he just waved that thought off with his hand, as if it had been a confusion, and walked away into the crowds, turning back once to give me a salute with his right index finger from the brim of his hat. I watched him—it was like all the right elements for him, for he appeared taller than ever, his lean form aloft of all the others swarming the gate, that white Stetson making its buoyant way up into the white lights as I followed it, and continuing, as if floating over the throngs pushing through and up the ramps, beyond the gate and up into the stadium itself, till all the whiteness and human massing and brightness of the great lighted Dome finally, far up there, swallowed him, and he was gone.

I drove out, along the empty exit lanes by all the rowed headlights of cars headed in, out into a city that seemed momentarily empty outside, and dark. "If you can't like," he had said. And I was feeling on his midnight train to nowhere, and he had gotten off, and now I too had to find the lights, the make-believe, whatever it was that it took to like. To survive as he did. The birds could screech by the millions in the darkness, and the soul sink to infinite smallness, but that had to be only in passing by. It could not be the place where you stopped. Or you were dead. He had said something like that. You were dead.

I headed back up Kirby toward Main. I was still seeing that Stetson floating into whiteness, reclaiming itself in the hurry and humanity of this world, the living, the lights that might, I realized, be the only conceivable stop short of nowhere. And abruptly I heard the radio, it seemed for the first time. The dispatch was dispensing trips.

I set myself to grab one.

Medusa

I had dropped off out San Antonio Road that evening, a little-known byway in the near vicinity of the port that poked its way north from Lawndale into an isolated cluster of back lanes and railroad tracks with the daunting look of a maze in the Key Map. I had never been to this corner of Houston before, tucked up in a great looping bend of Brays Bayou on its eastward course for the Channel, yet knew it from local history as the site of the earliest settlement in the area, the lost village of Harrisburg that had even served briefly as the Texas capital during the Revolution. Burned to the ground by Santa Anna's army just days before San Jacinto, and then rebuilt only to be bypassed by the founding of Houston itself five miles further west, Harrisburg to my surprise still seemed more a relic of its frontier past, a ghost town, than a working class district beside one of the busiest waterfronts in the modern world. And even more forlorn in the trailing mist swarming over the blackness of its reaches—spawned since nightfall by the sudden return of cooler temperature after days of unseasonably warm, early spring rain had soaked the city—a silent drift of vapors alternately obscuring and revealing the abandonment of Harrisburg's blank and shambling facades in eerie clouds and specters.

It seemed a night of the archaic. Even my passenger: an old Chicano gentleman sporting a vaquero's straw Stetson and wizened enough he might actually have worked cattle on the old range. And implacably still in the middle of the back seat, staring forward over my shoulder, all the way up from the southern outskirts of the city where I had picked him up at a market out Almeda Road, the shadow of his Stetson like a mysterious icon framed in my mirror.

Leaving him before what appeared to be the ruin of an old dry goods store, black and boarded up, where once he entered the creaky door I saw the glow of a hurricane lamp come alight through cracks in the structure, I elected to continue north and explore a little this neighborhood, impelled by the aura of history it contained, rather than return to Lawndale and west back into streets I was more familiar with as a new driver. Also I was thinking of a trip coming my way from further up in the East End, as just then I heard dispatch call Harrisburg 3, the precinct directly beyond Brays, though the trip was taken immediately from the precinct's cab stand, the driver told to go to the Latin World Nightclub.

I heard nothing else for the East End, however, and minutes later was on the verge of abandoning my odyssey anyway, backtracking to Lawndale in failure, as almost everywhere I turned I was forced back from one candy-striped barrier after another dead-ending my passage— either at the many tracks combing old Harrisburg in a baffling web, as if the city saw no need of RR crossings in such a deserted, forgotten place, or at the banks of Brays Bayou itself cutting short any other lanes I tried, its swollen waters riffling through the silence of the night from behind the gaunt limbs of trees arching out in grotesque patterns over the painted slats in my lights like something gothic in the fog, spooky. At last frustrated with bumping around in the dark, even thinking petulantly how characteristic this was of my life anymore, I chanced up a narrow road hugging one set of tracks, perhaps leading somewhere, and hit the accelerator rather hard. Suddenly out of the mist a horseman emerged galloping straight at my lights, a young Chicano tipping his Stetson at me as he adroitly tugged his reins to sidestep a collision, the hooves clopping by my cab and horse and rider vanishing like an apparition.

I gasped, glad I hadn't hit them, and stopped. The clip-clop of the hooves melted to silence out my open window.

I sat there, lost in the black wash of fog rolling over my cab, and white across my headlights, in the startled jangle of my nerves at the near miss succumbing again to consternation, still one more time among many the past two weeks, that I was actually here and doing this, that I wasn't in the Texas Medical Center earning an M.D. anymore, but here. And only adding to the dream it all seemed to be, was the memory now roused in my head, like a jolt from that improbable horseman just now vanished behind me, of the cowboy I too had once wanted to be, long ago when riding the sea lanes of childhood in my mother's anxious arms, the horseman I would be to impress her, save her some way from her worry over me—but a hope vanished, as so much of my childhood with it, once my physician father, so sure of what was best, took command of my upbringing and pointed me to medicine. The future, great things to be mine—likewise vanished now. And sitting there in a streaming of fog that almost seemed the world in vague, primordial times, it struck me how I'd really come full circle in a way, adrift in sea lanes all over again, but in the bosom now of this amphibious city claiming me like an orphan, this "Liquid City" as she was aptly called, that like a new mother was my nurturing now, following the metamorphosis that had so recently placed me here, behind the wheel of this cab: blurred, groping for a new sense of form in the dark world of the night driver, free—and still startled at being so—after a professional life and definition I had shed like so much skin that was just too tight to be possible anymore.

I drove on, the only thing possible. Determined to get on with my shift, trips to be had, out of this blackest of places where time, in the long ago, seemed suspended, stopped.

Lights appeared to my right, a congregation of houses, families in them, and in grateful relief at what felt like rescue, I made Broadway, and was northbound up the Broadway Viaduct into the East End when I heard dispatch call Harrisburg 3 again, only to throw it open this time when no one answered from the cab stand. Grabbing my mike with a swift "621" in response, I was asked immediately my position, which was unusual. Apparently satisfied I was close enough, dispatch awarded me the trip. But even stranger were the instructions. I was told to go to the Latin World Nightclub, on Harrisburg Boulevard directly ahead, but to meet the other yellow cab that had been assigned there earlier. The other cabby, for reasons not specified, needed to transfer the fare he had picked up.

I was there quickly, arriving at 8:55 PM as I noted in my

log, a time when the Latin World, one of the largest Hispanic clubs in the city, was heating up. The parking lot was full, but I found the other cab in a corner and pulled up close by. A woman sat on the passenger side of the front seat. The driver, a tall, attractive black, got out and came around to speak with me. He leaned in at my window. "She's a friend, a good friend, and I can't charge her, you see. When I found out who my fare was I just called for another cab. With your number, who knows, maybe you're the right one. 621—it's amazing. But there's no problem, no problem at all, I assure you. She's a beautiful lady. Just take good care of her."

"My pleasure," I nodded, though certainly confused at the mention of my number—what had that to do with it?—and a moment later, after a few last words with the driver, the woman left his cab. But she stopped outside mine. She seemed to be looking at my number on the side of the vehicle, in thought for a moment, before finally opening the door and slipping in the front seat beside me. She was a Chicana in her late twenties or so, a slim woman with black hair in a Dutch Boy cut, and a dark face out of which the pools of her eyes gleamed with an uncanny brightness as she fixed them on me after closing the door. A handsome, strong countenance, if not beautiful, for her skin was not delicate and smooth, but roughened slightly, patchy, and lacked make-up. Yet the high cheekbones and ruggedness of her face seemed only a frame for the bizarre glow of her eyes, like two penlights shining at me in the dark of the cab.

I shuffled nervously under their stare. They studied me for a long moment, until finally I had to look away.

"Thank you for taking me," she said, in a voice rather

tired and restrained as she turned to adjust herself in her seat. "Johnny said he explained to you why he couldn't. It's a point of honor with him not to charge a friend. It's for the best, I realize now. I'm staying at a place off the west end of Navigation. Just head that way on Harrisburg till I show you where to turn."

The meter flag over, I eased through the parking lot and into the traffic of Harrisburg. "That's quite a coincidence," I said, trying to shake off the impression of her eyes, "to end up with a driver who's a close friend—I mean, out of all the drivers who work this city."

"No. No. Not in my case." Her voice sounded even more exhausted. "I was a driver for Yellow Cab. I drove nights for five years. I know many of the drivers, the veterans at least."

"Oh really," I said in surprise.

"Yes. It's what I loved to do." She wore a simple brown dress, and held her hands demurely in her lap, clutching a little purse. But her modest demeanor, and the slow, fatigued tone of her voice, were belied altogether by those eyes, that again I saw studying me. "In fact, you're driving my number."

"What? 621?"

"Yes. My number. For all five years. Though this is a new Plymouth they've assigned you."

A note of grief just audible in the way she said this caught me short, and despite my urge to say something again about coincidence—there were several hundred cabs in the fleet—I dropped it.

She turned from me to look forward again. But I saw her quiver slightly, her eyes shut a moment, as if trying to fight back the feeling she'd betrayed.

We came to a stop at the 69th Street light. Harrisburg was busy this time of night, a lot of people out in cars or crowding the walks between a helter-skelter of taco joints and markets and bars flanking the street and blaring cheap neon in a garish melt, like crayon colors turned water in the foggy air. Out our open windows the chatter and shout of Spanish blended with mariachi music from speakers and radios in all directions, overlapping to a muted confusion of noise. But she seemed oblivious to it all, just staring into space beside me, gripping the purse in her lap.

"How was it for you, driving 621?" I asked, trying to make conversation as we sat backed up at the light. "Five years is a long time at this job. Did you make a good living?"

"Yes. Good money." She only glanced at me and then looked away again. "I was the best driver in the fleet, in fact. Top of the list for revenue almost every week. If I didn't make Driver of the Week it was usually because I had missed a night, because I was sick. . . or some other reason. It was especially hard for me the last two years."

The light changed and I pulled away. "Well, that's something I'll never be, Driver of the Week," I said, choosing to overlook her last remark. "I just started a couple of weeks ago, and was happy enough not to be at the bottom of the list when it came out. I'm sorry, but I guess 621's come down in the world. But why did you leave? Did you find another job?"

"No. Just what I said: it's what I loved to do. But Yellow Cab refused to hire me back today."

I wasn't sure what to say to that. Our passage was slow, the lights close together here. At 67th Street we sat stopped at another light, and though an intersection equally congested as those behind, with neon and crowds and bustle, I felt a kind of remove from it all because of this woman. I looked at her. But she remained staring ahead. In profile her short haircut made her look young. Or old, I couldn't tell. Only that she appeared tired, drained even, yet was pulled in tight against some agitation gnawing at her. "But had you quit before, was that it?" I ventured to ask.

"No. I never quit. I had to leave."

She turned to look at me.

"Had to—?"

"Yes." Her face was suddenly cold, stern. "I had to. You may as well know. I killed my husband. I was tried for murder, and sentenced."

The shine in her eyes was almost hideous that moment, glaring at me, like she was something from the dead and defied anything I might say or think in reply. Shuddering, I looked away at the stoplight, an excuse.

"How. . . how did you do that?" I asked, as the light changed.

"Easily."

She turned to look out her window, saying no more.

I took a few deep breaths, realizing I had never known a murderer before. But a woman? Her husband? We entered a more industrial sector of Harrisburg, warehouses and small plants, mainly closed for the night, and dark. Away from the nightlife behind us the traffic thinned, and I picked up speed. The fog thinned as well, and above the westward course of the boulevard downtown Houston hovered into view, a murky spangle of lights blotted across the misty night in nebulous phallic array.

"You don't seem the kind of person who could do that easily," I finally remarked, unable to tolerate the silence.

"How can you know? You're even uncomfortable to look me in the eyes. How can you know?"

"No. . . that's not true," I blurted. "I mean—"

"No, it *is* true," she said. She looked out her window a moment, then back at me. "But it's all right. Forgive me, you seem a sensitive young man. That was not fair of me, I'm sorry." A dry, exasperated chuckle escaped her. "Do you know these eyes were even used against me in court? The evidence was inadmissible, of course, but the damage done. Witnesses called to the stand, who said that I was evil because of these eyes. A *bruja* with the devil in her eyes, they said. And how many men in the barrio chased them once, wanting the challenge of conquering, subduing them. Not that one of them could actually look me in the eyes, face me. Though there was one finally I thought could. And I let him claim me.

"We'd been married two years. He didn't like me driving, had been making life difficult about it for a long time. But he got physical with me one night, started slapping me around when I was trying to get out the door to go to work. I stabbed him with the butcher knife in the kitchen. Our baby was crying in the next room when it happened."

"When was this?"

"Two and a half years ago. What time is it?"

I looked at my watch. "Just after 9 o'clock."

"I'm supposed to meet my parole officer at 9."

"Well, where is that? We better hustle."

"I'm not going. Just take me to where I told you. It's too late now. They'll come get me and take me back. I just want to go back." She was waving her head, emotion beginning to run up through her body and words, though she kept her hands clutched in her lap, holding the purse like it was her only center of gravity.

"Back to where?"

"Huntsville State Prison," she rasped out, through clenched teeth and parted lips of a suddenly monumental struggle with herself. She looked away, her whole body shaking. I heard her take a deep, steadying breath, crepitant with gasps she couldn't quite stop. "That's where I've been. The Goree Unit. But they let me out on parole last week for good behavior. I tried to get my job back, but was refused today. So there's nothing here for me."

"But what about your child?"

"He's with my husband's family. I can't get him back. Turn right at the next corner."

I had planned a right on Lockwood, a major boulevard further ahead, and more efficient for reaching her destination. But maybe she wanted to take longer. Turning where she directed, we entered the poorest and darkest streets of this sector of the barrio. I was forced to slow way down over the bumpy, broken pavement. In the liquid night the few and feeble lights of an occasional window or screen door seemed uncertain pockets of life along our way, not quite rooted in the dilapidated tangle of houses, but floating. The drift of moisture swayed across my headlights in shreds of fog.

"I grew up here," she said. "In these streets I was known as *La Taxista*, the Cab Lady. Feared, yes—I was so different from any of the women of the barrio—but respected. Now I am only hated here. You should have seen them pack the courtroom to watch my trial."

"Well, you can live elsewhere. You're clearly capable. Look, let's go find your parole officer. I can argue I just got lost trying to get you there."

"Cross Canal Street up ahead, and go on up to Navigation. You can make a left there."

"How can driving be the only thing you can do?"

"You don't understand, you can't. For most of you cab driving is just a passing thing. You come and you go. But it was a life for me. The. . . the control, the command of it. A way to take charge. And I, a woman. This city was my city. At least at night, it was mine. No, more—but how can you understand?—this city, you see, it *was me*," she said, in defiant, breathy emphasis of these last words.

"Maybe you're finding out for yourself," she continued, "but it's not a life where anyone can say 'no' to you. The trips are yours as you seek them, and once you earn a trip, have a destination, the decisions are all yours. There's no 'no' to it. You realize how much 'no' there is to life? I just can't stand it, can't live that way."

"But prison—"

"And my husband," she interrupted, "that's all he was in the end. This is Canal. You need to go to the left or right to cross."

I jogged way over to the left, as the cross streets along this stretch of Canal didn't match up, but were all askew of one another in an odd confounding of any plan. Then it was up another dark lane of vapor and gloom.

"You know, he promised me he would never make an issue of my driving. When we were engaged. He promised me. I refused to go ahead with the engagement unless he did. He was a handsome man, and seemed free-spirited, especially for a Chicano. He could laugh." She stopped, sinking in on herself and looking out her window. Her voice was dry, flat, but I wondered if she needed really to cry, with the memories that burdened her, if she had even talked with anyone in a long time. I looked at the back of her head, that short black hair in its prison cut.

"But what does marriage do to a man?" she went on, looking back at me. "How it changed him. It was hard, I know, that I went off to work as soon as he got home, and he went off to work as soon as I got home. We had only two nights a week together. I gave up driving six nights. But he started complaining, and began to drink. Even before the baby was born. I kept driving, even though I was pregnant. I wouldn't give it up. Then, after the baby, it became impossible. I couldn't leave till he was home, till he could be with the baby. He took advantage of that, coming in late some nights, and drunk, so I couldn't even go to work because the night was half gone and I couldn't leave him alone with the baby like that. Then other times, when he did come home on time, he just took the baby to his sister's the moment I left, and got drunk anyway. I would have to go to his sister's the next morning to pick up my child. They already hated me over there, so I dreaded going, to be forced to ask for my baby back like that. Turn left here."

I had reached Navigation, a wide boulevard fronted by warehouses long since closed and deserted this hour, dreary in their dark bulk. I turned up between them, my headlights tunneling even denser vapor this close to Buffalo Bayou winding on our north toward the Ship Channel behind us. Activity was around the clock back there along the docks, but here, going the other way, we were alone.

"The night it happened he came in late again, and not only drunk, but angry, yelling. I too was angry. It was one more night I had had to call into the lot, and cancel. It was becoming humiliating to make that call. I then decided I was going to work anyway; I was tired of him running my life like that. But he got all out of control, yelling I had to quit. He would no longer have his wife exposed the way I was to other men. It was a man's job to drive a cab, and he was putting his foot down. I had to be at home all the time from now on, for him, for the child. Had to be a wife, a wife, a wife—"

She shook her head fiercely at the memory. "He slapped me every time he said it. A wife. Slap, slap. The knife was there on the cupboard. It's amazing really, how easy it was. I just did it. Right into the heart. I kept it sharp, but I didn't know you could penetrate the chest that easy."

I drove slowly, only a semi now and then headed the other way, with cargo for the docks, roaring by and leaving us again in quiet. She just stared ahead now, into the blank vapor rolling up our headlights, her hands still in her lap, clutching her little purse. I realized how girlish she looked that way, young.

A girl. One of the Goree Girls. I had heard the women inmates at Huntsville referred to that way.

"Did the company explain why they wouldn't hire you back?" I asked. Maybe a pointless question, but I wanted her to keep talking. We were not far now.

"He didn't want to talk to me. He'd been the manager

back when I drove. He knew how good a driver I'd been, at least before I married. That I had made money for them. But he didn't want to talk to me. He refused to see me for a week; I'd been calling since I came back into town. Finally I just walked in on him this morning, tired of being put off. You could see he dreaded having me in his office. He grabbed my file and all he could do was harp on one incident. It had come up at my trial, and he knew it. He had supplied the story himself to the prosecution.

"I had picked up at a bar late. The man, a middle-aged Anglo, was drunk, and leering at me as soon as he was in the cab. He stunk of liquor and made coarse remarks, then something about my eyes, all the time inching closer and closer. I'm left-handed, and when he finally put his hands on me, trying to fondle me even as I was driving, I just let fly across the steering wheel with my left, smack in his face. I hit him again and again, not losing control of the cab, but furious. I had just married, I had my wedding ring on and it tore up his face too. I never told my husband, of course, at that time to protect him from worry. The man was really stunned; he was too drunk to fight anyway and I hit him hard. I was able to pull over, he was so dazed, and actually come around and drag him out of the passenger side, with more punches to his face and a knee to his groin that dropped him on the curb. I left him there, and immediately drove to the lot to report the incident. The next morning a man called to complain a woman driver had pulled a gun on him and forced him out. He couldn't identify the cab, but there were only two other women driving nights back then, and when he said she had strange eyes it was clear who he was talking about. But the fact I had reported the matter, and the man disappeared—didn't press charges, but just vanished—as well as my good record with the company, probably is what saved my job. And I don't carry a gun, he would have had to prove that. But the incident was in my file.

"That's what the manager kept on about. That I might harm a passenger. Like I had killed my husband—he added that too. But he wouldn't look at me the whole time. I argued, pleaded with him—my record overall, the revenue I had brought the company, and that the incident he talked of was just self-defense. He became really uncomfortable, finally claimed the police wouldn't approve my hire anyway. When I said the company should stand up for me he blew up, got out of his chair and yelled at me that I was a 'snake', a 'snake'. He shrieked it, again and again, so everyone in the building could hear, yelling I could take my 'fangs' and my 'evil eyes' elsewhere—his words too—and to get out. When I walked out he slammed the door behind me, yelling 'bitch'." She was breathing hard as she finished, seething, yet defeated it seemed by that insult capping off her effort at parole.

"Look, forget him. Let the past be. You can change, be someone else. Let's go find your parole officer, please." I was driving even slower. "Please, there's no reason to go back to prison because of this."

"No, no. You don't understand."

"Look, please listen. Maybe I understand more than you realize. Several months ago you know where I was? I was wearing a white coat, stethoscope in pocket, walking the wards of Ben Taub Hospital trying to learn to be a doctor. But it was all technical. I couldn't find the human. Maybe it's stupid, there's so much humanity in medicine, but I couldn't find it myself. I just wanted people in an immediate kind of way. But it was all bright technology and tubes and needles, and I was terribly unhappy. And then. . . I threw it away. Years of preparation, and I threw it away. So here I am, doing this instead. I ferry people now, as you did. I'm 621 now. As you were. But it's change I'm talking about. Asserting yourself, as you ultimately asserted yourself in that kitchen, even if wrong, or at least judged wrong. I'm my own jury; you had one imposed on you. But it comes down to the fact we have to change in the face of judgment, adapt for ourselves. Maybe become more primitive even, lose a sense of definition, of identity for a while—but change, and work toward something new." I ceased, suddenly embarrassed I had run on like that. Could there be any equation in our circumstances? And there was still so little sense to it anyway, what I had done, that I could feel closer to life doing this than in medicine. The sick I had abandoned, the many sick over the years I could have helped. And this woman, who seemed so healthy to me, I couldn't help one jot.

We were at a point where Navigation dips south toward Canal, an area of tenements creeping in among the warehouses, with downtown Houston a liquid of glitter, like a drowned Atlantis, reaching high overhead in the near distance.

"It's here," she said quietly. "Slow up. Make the next right." I did. "Stop. This is good."

We were facing down a rutted, dead-end lane. The shadow of a crumbling two-story house stood to the right, banked in weeds that ranged into my headlights. I turned off the meter.

"What time is it?" she asked.

"9:20."

"I'll just wait. They won't be long coming, I'm sure."

"But how can you stand incarceration, when you don't have to? How can you stand prison?"

She sighed, long and slowly into the cab, looking down my headlights that ended in nothing but a black tangle of undergrowth peeking with new foliage. I even thought I smelled a hint of jasmine, somewhere in there beginning to bloom. "Maybe it's easier, that's all, if you choose it," she said. "You made your choice, what you just told me about. And you don't seem to be sure it's the best decision, but you made it. I just don't know what else to do. I can't stand it being out, that's all. The only hope I had was getting my job back. Otherwise I. . . I don't know how to bear it. Can you understand? And prison, you might be surprised, is easier than you think. It's just you and yourself alone—not all this out here, like a pressure right now I. . . I just can't handle.

"The hardest thing for me was trying to see that manager, being told by his secretary, 'No, no time. He has no time for you now.' And then having to walk in on him like that, plead, and endure his humiliating me. If anyone humiliates me again it will be me, and me alone. I debated all day today after that meeting, all over again, what to do, just sitting up there, behind the window, staring at the skyline in the rain and feeling this pressure in me I didn't know what to do with. I had to make a decision. I was still debating what to do at the Latin World when 9 o'clock approached and I called a cab. I was hating myself, afraid I would say, 'Take me to this address I have in my pocketbook.' That I would go see that parole officer after all, endure his smiling and condescension. And out of the blue it was Johnny, who wouldn't take me. His 'point of honor' as he called it. So the address never even came up. Then out of the blue it was the cab with my old number. Right there beside us. Johnny recognized it too, and I knew he felt sorry for me. I had told him I hadn't gotten my job back. But I hated it, how he felt sorry for me, and then, looking at 621 on the side of your cab, just seemed to make the decision for me. I've lost this world I wanted back; I don't have it anymore. I've lost 621, it's not mine anymore. But I have. . . have at least me. *Me*, do you understand?" she said volubly, her eyes a penetrating flash in that instant of hard exasperation. "I can feel some. . . some something at least that I am choosing this. And you, and your cab, that was the last cab I ever expected, helped make it that I could choose what I had to choose. Without you I wouldn't be going back, I think. But I'm glad. Can you understand? I'm glad."

"So, I'm both a usurper and an accomplice, that's what you're telling me." I looked at her. "Well, I'll try to take it as a 'point of honor' that I'm your accomplice." But I was all bewilderment, my attempt at sarcasm flat.

"But you see, and you must understand this," she said with feeling, "that's something I never had before: an *accomplice*. And I think what this means is that I can change. But I've got to go back first, go back in order to do it. This time there'll be no dreams of returning to what I once had. I have to shed it, shed it all, and maybe I can start over. So please, do take it as a point of honor what you have done for me.

Please." And she grabbed my hand across the seat between us, looking deep into my eyes from the deep light of her own. And that moment, from the emotion evident in her face, and the impulsive grip of her hand on mine, its tenderness, it seemed to me the glow in her eyes grew brighter, deepened, to clarity, to definition. I saw a young woman there, and that she was beautiful. In another context I could have kissed her, courted her. Even married her.

She removed her hand. "Here's your fare." She pulled the money from her small purse. "I can only afford a small tip, I'm sorry. I wish it could be more."

"Can you start over?"

"I'll get parole again, someday." She pushed her door open. "Goodbye. I wish you well, please know that. Goodbye."

She got out of the cab. I wanted something more to say, but there was nothing. She was walking away, along the edge of my headlights, then veered to the right, into the darkness beside a set of stairs I could vaguely make out leading up the side of the house to the second floor. The smell of jasmine was stronger now to my nostrils, from the undergrowth beyond. Then I saw them, looking at me from the dark: two points of light, her eyes, like an animal's reflecting a torch-light. Then her steps quickly up the wooden stairs, and a door slamming in the night.

Metal

The neon of The Pink Panther was a soft sherbet glow against the dark of the late night. It was nearly 2 AM, closing time, but a mirthful hubbub mixed with juke box country western muted its way through the closed door of the premises and rose up into the pink neon to cast a cotton candy aura of carnival cheer over the deserted street. Here in the lower corner of downtown the buildings were old and low, revealing a broad sky that seemed to pull the fluorescence of the bar's neon far up into itself and dissolve it in the high moisture of the Gulf, making the stars appear like tiny gems shining up from the black bottom of a pool touched ever so slightly in pellucid, simple radiance of pink.

It was a man's bar, but pink, and the passengers I had picked up here were always working men who brought out the door with them a kind of kid's love for wide skies and high stars, and the romance of roughneck Houston. Buoyed on beer and hopes they talked—of the basic tasks ahead in the day, more often than not some crazy, rush job they complained of but were tacitly proud of; of women, their wives usually; or of aspirations born in the simple economy of work and livelihood: maybe a boat they wanted to buy, or a fishing trip they wanted to take, or a birthday gift for a son.

I drove them home, where they could get some sleep and bring it all into reality the next day.

Comfortable, with the swagger of an old-timer, I passed through the door and into the vivid pink decor, where a crowd of late drinkers at the bar and the many little tables seemed to notice me amicably out of their general, pleasant confusion of talk and music and last drinks before closing time.

"Cab," I said easily to the familiar bartender wiping his rag vigorously over the counter. He gave me an odd half smile, though, a kind of anxiousness in his brow, and cocked his head over toward the far corner of the room.

"Yeah, he's over there," he said. "I'll let him know."

I walked back outside, making no attempt to see who the individual might be, but in full confidence I would enjoy another conversation with someone who only five hours from now would be working up a refinery tower, or along the docks of the Channel, or atop a production platform in construction out Greens Bayou. Someone who made this city hum where it really counted.

I was in a reverie of stars, staring out my window where I had parked in front, when I heard a sudden jump in the music's volume and bar's chatter reach the street, then mute just as abruptly as the bar door swung closed again. He was opening the front door of the cab as I turned, a figure stout and hunched, with a big face. He pushed his way into the front seat beside me. I thought immediately he looked just the way I always imagined Dr. Jekyll's Mr. Hyde to look. "Evening," I said, somewhat startled at the face with a broad, ugly grin staring at me, the cab door still wide open behind him. "Well, pull that door shut and we'll be off. Where you going?"

He turned and found the door handle, and slammed the cab shut. "Out North Main. Near Airline." His voice was gruff, throaty, like that of a dwarf, which he wasn't. A full-size version of Rumpelstiltskin, or a Mr. Hyde. I didn't know who it was I had in my cab, but he continued to grin at me in a pleased, salacious way as I pushed the meter flag over and pulled away from the curb. His thick black hair seemed slicked with sweat. There was an excitement about him, as if he were charged up with anticipation and I was the object. He had carried a jacket with him, which crossed his left thigh, but strangely he had his right hand under it.

I circled back toward Main, and turned north. Downtown Houston was a vacated place now, but my passenger made me jumpy enough to welcome the lights of the city's center, though they burned over sidewalks without a soul on them. I did not, however, welcome the destination for this trip: a derelict neighborhood well to the north, always eerie at this hour.

Everything about him was a concentration on me. He never once took his eyes off me, or wiped that expectant, self-assured grin from his face. And his right hand never stirred from beneath that jacket.

"What if I told you I had a gun pointed right at you?"

He said it slowly, calmly, but as I looked abruptly at him I saw his eyes bulged eagerly from his face. His grin broadened into a perverse smile—pleased with the character of my surprise he even nodded his head slightly. I glanced up Main. Running precision-straight between high lampposts

41

bearing huge, bright-white globes, for a vanishing point that fairly glowed in a skein of mist at the far end, downtown Main presented an exquisite lesson in perspective this hour of the night. Like a highway to heaven. But utterly empty at 2 AM. Not a police car anywhere in sight, or a pedestrian, or anyone.

Just perspective, and a street.

"I would wonder why you are doing that. You can have my money, if that's what you want."

"That's not what I want."

"What is it you do want?"

"But that's for you to find out, isn't it? Oh, and it is loaded. The trigger feels very round and snug in my finger. I like the feeling of metal. Cold, curved metal, that carries power in it. Don't you agree? There's nothing that feels quite like it."

We were rolling through the lights, timed perfectly to keep us in a brisk passage for the real terminus of this galactic, deserted highway: the Main Street Viaduct over the Buffalo Bayou. That bridge marked the border of all comfort I otherwise felt on this street. Beyond it Main dipped down and entered an unwholesome part of the city, became increasingly dark, narrow, until. . . where he was going you would never walk alone at night without being very alert, or even drive if you could help it.

What *did* he want? I had broken out in a quiet sweat, cold like the metal he talked of.

"I have never understood why people liked guns," I said, in a strained, tight voice. Some impulse urged me to engage him in conversation. Besides, was that gun bona fide? He wouldn't show it to me, so maybe he was just playing games.

I didn't know. It could have been a pop gun or a candy cane. I didn't know.

"Because most things deserve a gun pointed at them."

The two white rows of streetlamps no longer closed toward a point of perspective, but opened, wider and wider and black, like a gateway now to a nether world. We were through it and up onto the Main Street Viaduct, arched over the slow, dark waters of the bayou below. I caught only the slightest glint of surface between the jungled shadows of banks tumbling steeply from the high ridge of warehouses each side. We passed the black, factory-like structure of the old M&M Building guarding the north bank.

"Why do most things deserve a gun pointed at them?" He had been waiting patiently for my reply, never once altering in any way his eyes, or posture, or grin. I had his undivided attention, and that of something held in perfect stillness beneath his jacket.

"You mean you drive around this city every night and can't answer that?"

"Well, maybe things still need a chance. It's hard to function with a gun pointed at you."

"You seem to be doing a pretty good job of it. Too good." He let that sink in, then continued in a voice betraying just the slightest edge of aggravation in its slow, cold rebuff. "I don't see why things need any chance at all. It's damn near remarkable and disgusting you think that. They've had plenty of chance, mister, and look what we've got for it."

"What do we have?" My voice was very tight, just barely escaping my throat. We were in a tunnel beneath the

Southern Pacific R.R. Yard, a constrained, claustrophobic space, as if pressed in by all the weight of the engines and freight cars and iron bulk above.

"We have Armageddon, mister, that's what we have. The world with a barrel down its throat, loaded and just waiting to discharge. A grand blow job on metal, that's what we have. But it's a world too tired and sick, and stupid, to pull the trigger, to even *know* to pull the trigger. Someone else is needed—it always seems to come to that—just to have the guts, the simple guts, to pull the trigger."

We exited the tunnel, bringing us abruptly into one of the large Hispanic districts of the city. Young men roamed about in groups, like shades, undefined in the vague light, in a pushing and shoving everywhere up and down the street, and shouts of frenetic, staccato Spanish that were unintelligible to me. The sleazy clubs of this slicked-back crowd had just closed, spilling them about in an obsessive search somewhere for something to do they had yet to figure. They moved in constant, blurred arrest, shoving up against the end of a block and turning back on themselves, gaining momentum only toward a volatile and meaningless denouement in knife blades and machismo. I drove by, fast and straight and not caring.

"Are you then some kind of perverse Messiah?" I said, in an exasperated moment of not caring what I said. "Going to save the world by pulling a trigger?"

"On the contrary, mister, I have no interest in saving a thing. Don't demean me by such a stupid idea." But his cold, offended tone suddenly gave way to more voluble irritation. "All you have to do is look at this sorry sight of jackoffs around us now. You really think anyone can have an interest in 'saving' this farce? Look at them, clamoring for honor against anyone and everyone because they're boozed up and stupid. Then they'll start drawing blood in some puny act of saving face. If they had some real guts—but they don't. They think they want to live. God, look at them. They think there's some kind of principle to uphold, but they don't know what it is. Some kind of faith that they're important, but they're trash. Here, run over one of them, why don't you."

I nearly did. A group loitering in the street went scattering to each side as I drove heartlessly through them, raising howls of execration in the wake of my taillights. Astonished I would do such a thing, I turned to my passenger, as if seeking an answer for it from him. A more relaxed, mirthful air had come back into his countenance, all grin again. "Not bad, but still chickenshit. You missed."

"I don't see the value in killing anyone," I erupted, now utterly aghast at myself. "What the hell purpose can it serve?"

"That's because you don't have the feeling of metal in your mouth. Blow job. But we'll take care of that. The feeling of metal down your throat the very moment the trigger is being squeezed. The barrel loaded, your teeth biting down in terror. I'm just you, you're just me—at that moment it doesn't matter, you see, who's who. We're one and the same: the ultimate copulation. *You* could pull the trigger even."

That grin grew wide and exalted in his face, a simple expansion of the pleasure now big and moist in his eyes. "You see, other people play with dicks. I play with guns."

"What's wrong with dicks? They're God-given."

"Oh, we have a smart one here. How did I land you?"

45

And he guffawed a moment. "Real good. That's real good, mister." Then suddenly his eyes were hard on me, the laugh gone. "Because dicks are impotent, that's why. It's Armageddon, remember? Metal's what it's about. Power. The only power."

"If it's Armageddon, why pull the trigger? Why a gun to end it?" Talk was breathing through me in a fresh initiative, the only recourse my sanity had against the crumbling of my composure. "Let this decrepit world die an old man, self-destruct in a dickless, impotent old age, a natural death it seems near to anyway in your thinking." Then I added impulsively: "There must be children around, to start things over."

"Not from this gentleman there aren't." Cold, he said that cold, looking steely at me, the grin vanished.

"I meant that as a metaphor."

"I know how you meant it. Don't treat me as stupid, mister. I've got you targeted, both up here," and he motioned with his left index finger at his head, "and down here," nodding at the invisible bulk in his right hand beneath the jacket.

Cab 621 rolled on, toward whatever it was awaited us. Beyond the blocks of Latin bars the buildings moved closer to the street, old, blank facades that were black through windows, or boarded over. The few streetlamps were pale, and cast a grey color. This area had a charnel quality, just from the sheer sense of dolor it evinced, as if buildings were barely outlasting people in a march to the grave.

"I'm not sure I know what it proves, that you can point a gun at me," I said in a voice dry, brittle, almost catching in my throat, but with a hint of irritation I couldn't mask. Maybe the tremendous fatigue this guy mounted on my soul was wearing the intimidation thin, but a seed of antagonism was taking root in the sordid climate of his insistent threats. Tears from it almost came into my eyes.

"It proves that things work from the barrel of metal. They happen. Not this slow, measly progression to nothing and nowhere that's the sorry state of things otherwise. So you want it to die of old age, do you, just drift off in a coma and—lights out? How boring you are, how boring. My God, history's been clamoring to tell us the truth for a long time. So we read about it in our books, we see it again and again on the screen, and we say, 'Oh, how unfortunate, we still don't have it right. Peace is what we want. War to end all war.' Well, there's only one way that can be. Armageddon, mister. Suck on metal. And pull, pull that trigger. And I've got one right here, mister, right here in my finger: smooth, curved, perfect. I never knew a tit that felt as good." He seemed moving toward some ecstatic moment as he spoke, his head wagging with his words, the gruffness of his voice thinned to a higher octave, his eyes alternately hard and moist with fever of his excitement.

"Does it give you a sexual high to intimidate people? I'm just curious." My matter-of-fact bluntness just came that way, I couldn't help it. It was as if he was forcing it from me, even against my will.

"You're stupid and presumptuous to think I'm *just* intimidating." He said it so slow, the hardness all back in him now, the eyes cold hatred, I knew I'd gone too far. Way too far. I trembled as I looked at him, then down at that jacket.

47

Desperate, I turned back to the road and the ordinariness of just driving. We were passing the Hollywood Cemetery, acres of statuary and high monuments for the dead pressing close to the street, a vast, ghoulish assemblage of shadows that almost seemed uprooted and moving, reaching for us, in my alarmed state of mind.

"I'm sorry," I muttered in a cowed and feeble voice. "I'm sorry. I'm just trying to know who you are, is all. Just trying to know. That's one reason I took up cab driving," I added, in some kind of vain reassurance in my own talk, "to know who people are. I don't drive around this city just taking tips and having fun, you realize."

"Well maybe I'll add a little entertainment after all, to whatever quixotic ideas you have driving this cab. Know who people are, hey? People, mister, are *dead*." If a word could be a thud, that last word was, like the thudding drop of a trap door, locking something in darkness. Final.

"Are you then... dead?" I couldn't help it. My tongue had a propensity for the seemingly stupid prod. My father raised me on Socrates. Even if it meant drinking hemlock someday, or maybe shortly. It was odd even: I felt I was already beyond whatever dire end this guy had designed for me, or was just playing at having designed (the thought it was a candy cane, months after Christmas, even jumped bizarrely back into my brain). I was already in a kind of limbo, he had taken me beyond. Or simply closed that trap door on me, so there was nothing but final darkness anyway to take affront at what I said.

"Mister, I was dead when God created this world. So was everybody else. We sleepwalk in the grave, and think it's life.

That's why we need a reminder. Metal. Suck on metal. Life is just death looking in a mirror and imagining. So give him something potent to imagine, something with balls in it. You got to suck hard, mister. Blow job. Or milk at the titties. It's the same thing. It's life, and never more than when you pull the trigger. It's the only dick or tit that counts, this sweet little thing in my hand. And it's feeling real good right now, kind of filling up right now, getting ready you know. Oh, my finger's getting itchy, I don't know, I don't know. . ."

Almost in a swoon that coarse voice, in its higher octave, and his eyes, they were not so focused, drifting, as I gaped in a surge of terror at him, his head huge and rolling it seemed on his hunched shoulders, his control evaporating in his rising ecstasy, his body relinquished to some incredible lust carrying him, about to heave him all into the pure, simple detonation of that gun. *Kingdom come. Thy will be done*, burst suddenly into my brain, from depths long forgotten of my mother's frequent praying over me. *Thy will*—and I was still over the wheel of a car moving, up Main, by acres of the dead. But something else drove it, my arms too shaky to steer.

He was moaning, in higher and higher waves of his abandonment, now drifting toward me. I nearly fainted in a crazed, ghastly fright. "Okay, okay!" I shouted helplessly. "Okay, whoever you are!" And he was bringing his right hand up, at my head, the jacket still drooped over what it held.

"Thy will be done," I babbled, shaking all out of control. His right arm was straight, pointed right at me.

I went convulsive. *"To kingdom co-o-o-me!"* I screamed, mouth gaping in a long choking sob of that last word, a paroxysm, my body that instant a violent discharge and shattering all over the wheel.

He had broken through. I was skying somewhere, completely separate, watching all this. I was an eye, the rest of me obliterated.

"That's better. Much better." He straightened himself up, his face subsiding from tension into that easy expansion of his grin again. "Much, much better. I think you got the feeling of metal in your mouth, mister. Doesn't it feel good?"

I was gasping, spent from all this, taking deep breaths to control myself. The wheel began to be real in my hands again. We crossed the North Freeway, far below us it seemed, with a few scattered headlights up and down its length. They were like the first live cars I had seen, life, other people in motion in this city. Then across, and Main became very narrow, in a neighborhood that was all but blacked out it was so dark and dismal. An old, boarded-up theater appeared ahead, its blank marquee like a cave entrance. "Stop here," he said. "Here!" he barked, when I merely slowed up. I stopped abruptly, short of the theater, and just stared straight ahead, like a rag doll, devoid of thought or purpose, of movement. No Socrates left in me, no questions or talk. Nothing. I had gone invisible. Only my body, it was all I felt, the mass that was me. Even time gone far, far asunder.

He threw a bill down. "You can turn the meter off." I did. "Incidentally, you were good. Very good. I've never had better. Also, incidentally. . . ," and he pulled from under his jacket a large pistol. I recognized it. A Colt 45 ACP. Army Combat Pistol, standard issue. He held it straight up in his hand, locking the safety in place with his right thumb as he kissed the barrel. "Just wanted you to know how close you were. But you were good. Very good. Never had better, really."

He opened the door and pushed his bulk slowly out, looking suddenly very tired. He stood briefly for a moment, as if collecting himself, in what was a deeply hunched posture over the sidewalk, then, shoving the door shut, he moved on, in a kind of forward and side falling motion that came into the penumbra of my headlights. He looked an unwieldy beast that way, trying to walk on its back legs but forced to push off its front legs to get back up straight again, then leaning off sideways when it did, tottering and falling forward again.

He moved on by the theater and was gone. Or did he go in? He was just gone. My headlights burned blank down a blank street.

Vietnam. It just hit me then. Vietnam. I don't know. That pistol, and something of the dialectician in me, maybe, trying to make sense. That busted body, hunched over itself. But veteran or no, he was gone. I was headed back, into brightness, hustling to find the North Freeway entrance, headed south and back. To the city, perspective, dawn approaching.

Carmen

I was called to an address on W. Alabama early one evening, when the cool of Houston's short spring still lingered, and the sun slanted down the length of the street in a wash of color. It was an old-fashioned neighborhood, of modest two-story homes in stone or brick masonry, with steep roofs and spindly chimneys, little porches, clipped azaleas and altheas on each side of the entrance, and small, well cared-for lawns reaching to the curb. Everything was bordered and trim, and diminutive: the tight driveways to tiny garages in back, the flagged walkways leading petitely to the porch, the tidy flowers and shrubs, and the rather stolid but narrow architecture of the houses themselves, like life was on a miniature scale for the sake of moderation and meticulousness.

But the address proved to be an entertainment agency, though the sign was modest enough beside the front door. I thought it odd such a business would be located here, but rang the doorbell and immediately set in motion a conversation carried up and down the stairs toward the back of the house and audible through the screen door. "Carmen, hurry up damnit, the cab is here" (shouted up the staircase by a burly figure I could barely make out from the glare of the sun on the screen). "There's plenty of time; tell him to wait" (a woman's more distant voice coming down the staircase). "Hell if there's plenty of time. You're on assignment, you know that, and that asshole expects you on time. We're paid for you to be on time, so hurry up" (up the staircase, the figure banging his hand hard on the balustrade). "We're paid, honey, for me to perform. He gets his money's worth from me. I'll be five minutes."

"Damn, Carm, you're going to stretch everyone's patience just a little too far someday."

"Honey, I'm paid to stretch things, remember? The further, the better. Now stop bothering me. You're interrupting my make-up."

The figure emerged at the screen, big, with cropped beard, and an irascible glint in his eye. "You'll have to wait, I'm sorry. She's a slow bitch until the sun goes down. There's no helping it."

I returned to my cab to wait, wondering what kind of entertainment was her *métier*. Were we headed to a theater, or some kind of cabaret back in Houston's old quarter off Market Square? The sun went down, in a glorious spangle of reds and cloud behind the silhouette of a Chinese tallow tree down the street. Shade came to the neighborhood, and a deeper cool in the air rising from the moisture of grass and shrubs after an earlier rainfall in the day. I was breathing it in pleasantly, thrumming my fingers on the dash, when suddenly I heard the screen door bang, and high heels click on the stone flags of the walk. I turned to see a buxom young lady miniskirted in black and swinging a black purse by the shoulder strap, in black blouse and with black, full-bodied hair to the shoulders, quick stepping in her black heels to the cab. She slipped into the front seat with a fluid shifting of body and smile that rocketed with her perfume right up into my wide eyes and set the pulse fast apace. "The Crystal Pistol, honey. No time to lose."

The Crystal Pistol. I would be called there later, after midnight, still reverberating from the waves crashing ashore of my male arousal from the ocean of presence she had been just a few feet from me on that fair ride. I didn't care the place was pure honky-tonk, just outside the Loop off South Main. Whatever she did there was fully excused as far as I was concerned. Her earrings dangled and swung ever so slightly to her breathing, almost hypnotizing me as I locked into staring at them at one stoplight. "Honey, I know you like what you see. But we've got to mosey. The light's green." I drifted back to the light and South Main's corridor of newly awakened neon stretching far and straight into the young night, her black eyebrows beside me etched in my mind like archways upon a Dali saturnalia of wild fluorescent color and fields of delectation where her body galloped, played with me. Her eyes and lashes, her earrings, sparkled in the rising brightness of city lights, she seemed to soak in and recreate the light as her own, an immanence all the more brilliant on my senses for the overwhelming character of black that was her attire, and her hair, and I knew, I think already then, her soul.

I opened the door of the Pistol and was greeted by loud Beatles (*Sgt. Pepper's Lonely Hearts Club Band*) and smoke curling everywhere in a shimmering, clogging haze, through which I saw none other than her friendly face gazing back at me from a central table in the crowded room. Beside her sat an elegantly dressed, elderly Latino gentleman, million-dollar Mexico City maybe, and he was leaning into her ear with talk.

"Honey," she shouted, "you're far too early to pick me up. Why, the night has only just started, now hasn't it, Mister Señor Mex? Or is it Macho? What is your name?" He looked baffled by this, then a little irritated, muttering something in Spanish and giving me a dirty look. I just waved to her and looked up at the bartender, who signaled yes, there was somebody, and I could wait outside. But possibly her dreamy, abstracted face, behind the cigarette held in her hand drifting smoke across her glittering eyes, or maybe the silver cage in the corner with a near nude lady working out the rhythms and metaphysics of "Strawberry Fields" in slow, writhing torsions of the body that looked like she was pulling entire shrubs and grasses and flowers right out of the floor at her feet (though her face was hidden behind the forward falling locks of her hair), maybe the fact that everyone, at all the tables, except Señor Mex (or Macho), who had his intentions clear, seemed vaporous and not quite of the body, but of substance abuse, I don't know, but I just stood there and looked the scene over.

"So, honey," she continued, beckoning me over, "there's no need to worry. Men need petting, is all, and that's my job, my specialty. How else are their frail egos going to be able to go out the next day and rob the world all over again of all its dreams?" She was propping her dreamy head up on her elbow, gazing up at me through those long lashes. "Twice in one night. That's almost a sign in a city this size. Oh, it looks like you have your fare." He had come out of the men's room at the back, a youngish big guy looking at me sternly as I stood in rapture at that woman's face, who winked at me. "Adios, amigo. Can't keep the customers waiting, you know. Maybe again, who knows. In a city this size all things are still possible, and what do they say about three times, three's the—ouch, Mex!" She jumped. The gentleman beside her had bitten her ear, trying to be tender about it, true (but teeth are teeth). He jumped back himself, alarmed at his faux pas, but she had begun reassuring him when I wheeled around and led my passenger out of the place.

From the Westheimer Two stand I was called at 4 AM to an address just a few blocks to the south. It was an old, grey apartment building, and I climbed to the second floor and walked down the length of a drab hallway with moths and assorted insects banging into the bare bulbs of the ceiling. The light was intolerably bright and glary to my eyes, and the blank doors facing in repeated monotonously the sense of enclosed, oppressive space the scene gave me. I imagined life locked away and moldering in the cubicles behind those doors. A surrealist setting for the corridors of hell, I thought, wondering who my passenger could possibly be at this hour in a dead place like this.

I found the door and knocked. Immediately it opened, and who else but Señor Mex, in white undershirt and boxer trunks looking at me disheveled and grey. And who else but . . . was tucking her black blouse into her black miniskirt beyond the bed behind him. But her back was turned. "Cab,"

I said to the gentleman quietly, who was apparently not million-dollar Mexico City after all, but a local Latino patron of life north of the border. But of course he recognized me, and sent me off to wait for her with a look more sad and resigned than irritable—though seeing me again seemed some kind of final defeat the way his old, paunchy body sagged in dismissal of me from his quarters.

I heard the fast click of her heels approaching. She bounced in. "Why, honey, you mean three times in one night? Now this beats all. There's definite karma here." And she gave me her address on Richmond, not far from where we were.

I swung the cab around and headed away. "It's an amazing coincidence, for sure," I said.

"Coincidence? No, honey. There's no such thing as coincidence. Things happen because they're meant to. This world's a pattern, don't kid yourself. It's just most people are too dumb or self-centered to see it. Of course, that's how I make my living, isn't it?—I'm a kind of cheat, after all. Men know nothing about patterns, only their peckers and how well they photograph, whether they're leader of the pack or will be shortly. I'm a cheat, you see, it's worth a couple of hundred a night. But seeing you three times now, that puts a little honesty in me again. Here, I tell you what, take my card," and she began rummaging in her purse. "Any time you want to talk real life, I'm your girl. Just please, none of the other stuff. A kiss, or a fuck, it's just business. But maybe somewhere there's a little poetry, hey?" She found the card. "Maybe you're a poet. We'll talk real life." And she gave me her card.

I tucked it in my shirt. And shortly I was tucking her fare, with generous tip, in my pocket, watching her click away into the darkness on those heels, swinging her purse by its shoulder strap, to vanish briskly beyond the portico where a sleek, black Corvette guarded the entrance to her place—located somewhere behind a line of tall azalea bushes in bloom, and one massive tangle of honeysuckle spinning the scent of its white blossoms in swirls of overpowering fragrance on the night.

I never answered her invitation. I even lost her card. Why, I wondered? Was she somehow only possible for me as the gypsy of The Crystal Pistol and bang, bang? To stroke my ego as she did every other man? I realized dismally I was afraid of the poetry in a woman whose soul was so black it soaked up all the light of this feeble universe of men, and emanated it as her own in celebration of something she called pattern. She was swinging her purse and clicking her heels on flagstones of some palace she called real life, and I was simply too awed to approach.

I never saw her again. The karma, with her card, was lost.

Africa

He flagged me down around 9 PM along Westheimer, and hopped in front saying he wanted to go to The Palace. A young, lean Latin in jeans and jacket, with a Roman nose and neatly combed, clipped black hair, he said he'd been told The Palace was the place to go. I noticed something bulging from under his jacket, tucked over his left breast. As we drove the few blocks to his destination I learned he was a Venezuelan sailor, from a ship due to leave port at 3:30 AM for Africa. But first he had business to attend to. "America is the land of business, is it not?" he said with a self-assured chuckle, leaning back with his left arm draped over the seat between us in a manner to make doubly evident the fact of some kind of cargo inside his jacket.

The Palace was a penthouse disco located atop an office building at 3400 Montrose, on the far side of a park from the Westheimer One cab stand. When waiting in line at the stand we would often gaze up at the staccato bursts of primary colors electrifying the interior of the penthouse, but only reaching us in a kind of dreamy quiet over the trees, the eerie silence of the reds, blues, and yellows flashing kaleidoscopically into the night somewhat akin to the soundlessness of an electrical storm lighting up great heaps of cumulonimbus far, far away over the dark prairie. For only up close to 3400 could you hear the muffled rock music held tight at high volume within the thick, well-insulated dark windows that walled in The Palace high above, only then imbibe some sense of the hedonism at full tilt up there, where ear-splitting volume racked the flash-dance of bodies and set them free to the dithyrambs of The Doors, The Stones, Led Zeppelin, and Cream.

I pulled up beneath the club on the side street adjoining the park, under the protection of live oak trees lining the curb in a cozy umbrella of gnarled foliage that effectively bundled the muted acoustics to an even further atmospheric remove, as if The Palace were some floating kingdom of the night sky the tellurian presence of all these leaves pushed easily up and away like a balloon. My passenger suddenly unzipped his jacket partway and pulled out a large transparent bag stuffed full of a different, and illegal, leaf, promising a different kind of atmospheric remove.

"They gyrate up in the sky, but I bring them even more of heaven. But first I do business with you. It's high-grade Venezuelan, well over a pound. How much you want to buy?" He held the bag proudly for my inspection.

I declined politely, however, on the excuse I still had eight hours left on my shift, and if I were caught with any of his "heaven" aboard I not only would lose my job, but perforce could expect a mere two-year minimum prison sentence to boot. "Texas law, you know. Not really worth it, don't you think?"

He seemed surprised, and disappointed, but tucked the

bag back under his jacket with a shrug. "I guess I have to find those already in the sky, hey?" He paid his fare and got out. "Good night, señor." I watched him disappear through the glass doors leading to the elevator, then drove around to the cab stand on the other side of the park. I never doubted he would sell what he had, and quickly, up there in the Never-Never of The Palace, and sail considerably wealthier for Africa.

At 3:45 AM I was headed south on Main Street through the heart of downtown Houston. I had dropped off a fare out the East End, and was cruising slowly back toward the West-heimer district in idle enjoyment of Main's wide, straight corridor flanked by massive streetlamps illuminating fiercely the desertion of street and sidewalk. With the high shadows of the tall buildings rising behind them blanked by the glare, the great white globes in close succession gave the impression against the bottom stories of a Greek temple on a super scale, made all the bigger by the sheer absence everywhere visible in the brilliant light.

Then suddenly a shadow interrupted my reverie, a figure darting out from behind one of the black lampposts at least a block ahead and running right at me waving arms and shouting in the great silence of this place. Then I saw him grab for his chest, as if he had been shot. But he came pell-mell on, holding his hands over his left breast, still shouting. When he reached me he grabbed the door handle and flung himself in the front seat of the cab.

He had flagged me down a second time this night: my Venezuelan sailor. But there was no ease in his manner now.

"My ship. I have to get to my ship. Please hurry, señor."

"Where? Where?"

"Sinclair. Sinclair."

"The refinery?"

"Sí, sí . Hurry, my ship leaves at 3:30."

"But it's already 3:45."

"That's why I say, señor, we must hurry."

I was already on my way, but a long way it would be to the Sinclair Oil docks.

"We leave for Africa at 3:30."

"But it's 3:45."

"That's why. We must hurry. They don't wait."

"Then they've left."

"That's why. We must hurry. Go faster, faster, please."

With no time to check the Key Map I was calling dispatch to find out which access road off the Pasadena Freeway to take to Sinclair, my passenger was still short of breath and leaning like he was stricken into the dashboard, and the Greek temple of downtown Main, its peace in the arrest of time, had become a speedway, as I ran my Plymouth through red light after red light, trying to check against some lone car or pedestrian that might yet cross in front of me this hour, comprehend at the same moment the dispatcher talking back at me in irritated surprise I couldn't just look in the Key Map for directions, and somehow make it backwards in time for the sake of this desperate young man with his bag of heaven who had almost no hope of making passage now.

God! Christ! I thought, driving like I never believed myself capable, expecting squad cars to come screaming after me any moment. Why was I even doing it? And if caught sure to lose my job, my license, even land behind bars.

On the Gulf Freeway, southbound at 90 mph, edging 100. "My ship leaves at 3:30. Hurry, señor, hurry."

"But it's 3:50."

"That's why. Hurry, I'm telling you."

"But it's already left."

"That's why. That's why."

"But you won't make it."

"That's why. That's why."

Over 100 now, the lights of the few cars at normal speed in either direction now whizzing back past us like stars by a sci-fi spacecraft in warp.

"Please, señor. My ship leaves at 3:30. For Africa. My black shipmates who've been there say it's like going back to beginnings. They say I must see it, see Africa. Please hurry, hurry, señor. My life depends on it."

"But your ship's gone. You said they don't wait."

"That's why. Hurry, señor."

I was on the Pasadena Freeway, our exit not far, when suddenly he unzipped his jacket partway and pulled out the bag. He held it my way without looking at me. "Do you want to buy?" he said in an exhausted voice. "It's high-grade Venezuelan. Want to buy?"

It was fully as full as it had been seven hours earlier. I only declined again, racing down the wide expanse of lanes and looking several times in amazement at this gentleman, who continued to hold the bag at me even though he stared in a kind of swoon ahead. "Buy, señor. It's the best for quality," he said mechanically.

He looked impaled really, everything individual about

65

him now sucked away by this crazy, desperate trip for nothing.

"I'll die, señor," he said, dropping the bag in his lap.

At 4:03, after negotiating a confusion of industrial back streets, I finally rolled up to the locked gate of the Sinclair refinery. There was no guard. I couldn't get through. He tossed some money down and dashed from the cab, scaling the tall hurricane fence with the bag of pot still in his hand, jumping down the other side and running headlong into the darkness capped by a millionfold of lights climbing heaven-ward up the vents and stacks and towers of this humming city within a city—like a near galaxy of stars in the black Gulf sky, beneath which the night swallowed him up, with no evidence anywhere of a ship's lighted superstructure along the far docks still awaiting him. He would run himself breathless to an abandoned wharf.

Suddenly just like all of us he seemed. Gripping our bundle of dreams, in a mad dash, and not catching up with any of it. Time heartless and always faster, our bundle just a vain hope of ever catching up. Only an empty wharf for each of us in the end, the ship that would take us—to beginnings, reprieve—long since departed.

He was out there somewhere, alone, nowhere else to go. But I didn't wait around. I felt sorry for him. And still had somewhere to go, I too easily apologized to myself, turning round and gunning it out of there. Leaving him.

Objet d'Art

It was a dingy-looking place in the dead of night, certainly the worst piece of real estate on San Felipe. Within only a stone's throw the avenue widened and was off on a comfortable, westward course through posh River Oaks, where high, elegant homes trimmed the night to a thing gardened and wholesome for the sleep of the prosperous. But Houston's freedom from zoning had allowed an invasion here. The windowless front wall of the low, crude building boasted "XXXX" and "Topless" beneath a single glary bulb, and a shabby tree arched over it all lent a Satanic portal effect at least accidentally artistic in its sinister chiaroscuro. In my first month of driving I had already delivered a few passengers here, dilapidated males I found at other bars, the voyeur types whose breath stank of beer and smoke and who stumbled and coughed their way from my cab to that portal. But now I had someone to pick up here, at 2:00 AM, closing time by Texas law for all such premises.

Acid rock beat in muffled waves through the wall as I walked up. I pulled open the door just a little, and music jumped out at me in high, weird guitar octaves of shattering volume. A sullen fat man fronted me belligerently as I found myself hanging back at what I saw and heard through the half-open door. "Cab," I shouted over the decibels. "Someone called." He grunted, almost like a fart from his mouth, as he motioned me brusquely back out the door and shoved it closed in my face. But I had had a glimpse over his shoulder before he did so: of steel bars along the far wall, cages in the yellow, smoky light, and one naked lady inside one of them thrusting her G-stringed thighs out in rapid pulse to the shriek of the speakers, her arms pushing away from her bare and bouncing breasts in equal beat to the music, the reverse jerking of her body in this way making her look like a grotesque mechanical puppet, but her face frantic, wild beneath a tangle of strewn hair, as men all about the joint stared at her, gawked, from tables littered with long neck bottles and scatter of cigarette ash in soak of spilled, pooling beer.

I walked back to my cab and sat behind the wheel, nauseated for the moment as if I had drunk all that beer in there and smoked all that smoke. What was it with men, I wondered, that they liked naked women confined to cages: behind steel their smooth, silk flesh, exposed and made scared and thrusting, made to (that is, paid to) imitate the sex act as if it were a torment beating from their pumping bodies only pain and succumbing—as if they were tied in straps of steel, bound back and pried open, poised brutally that way by force of eyes and lust and exercise of power on the rack? What was it, this male fascination with binding, brutalizing with eyes, and more, to make her play-act the beast? For the moment I was hating being male, and at such a place.

The door to the joint opened and shut quickly, and out to the cab came a lithe young lady in tight jeans and khaki shirt. She slipped into the front seat, smiled gaily at me as she recited the address, and settled in comfortably as I shoved the meter flag over and pulled away. Her address was east through the city, in an old and racially mixed neighborhood on the perimeter of Houston's Third Ward. She was a spunky passenger, squirming with enthusiasm beside me, and the hint of musk perfume played pleasantly in my nostrils and refreshed the interior of the cab. Her khaki shirt was leisurely unbuttoned to a low point, inviting easy glimpses of her firm and sizably handsome breasts, between which hung a silver crucifix shining against her dark, supple skin. Curly brunette hair in a mass framed prodigally a distinctively feral look in the blackness of her eyebrows and long lashes, her black, shining eyes moist with pluck, and the high cheekbones of her olive-complexioned, alluring Creole face.

And she wanted to talk. She asked if I would look at some pictures, and pulled them from a packet in her purse. "I had a photographer, a professional, take pictures of me, for publicity. I'm looking for a better place, more pay, and I figured it was worth the investment. Here, I just got the prints this evening, tell me what you think." She passed them to me, as I drove unhurriedly through what was a modest residential area now long since sound asleep. The close houses behind little lawns gave our passage in the cab a cozy, pleasant insularity.

I was intrigued at this confidence she had in me, and glanced at the photos I held up in one hand as I drove with the other, catching a suggestive eyeful in the half-light afforded by a momentary streetlamp. In the renewed darkness beyond reach of the lamp I wasn't sure I had seen the photo properly. Certainly I hadn't. No way I could have seen that, I thought. "Here," she said, "turn on the overhead light. It won't affect your driving, I'm sure." So I did, and then came to a stoplight anyway, where I had no excuse not to feast on what was, yes, just what I thought I had seen.

She was lying back on a thick white rug, propped on her elbows and fully nude, her legs spread apart and bent back under her at the knees, inviting the eyes right to the picture's center, where her proud black pubic hair was stretched just enough for her red, silk-wet treasure to gleam through like a hot pearl in all that rich blackness between her thighs. Her breasts had been massaged to point proudly their nipples in two tall little towers, as she herself looked out from behind them with a tiger grin of a side-glance at the viewer.

"Well, what do you think? Look at the others. Oh, the light's changed."

Mama. That's all I could think. I started up, but struggled to get my eyes back to where they had to be not to drive off the road. I slowed way down to slip through the rest of the photos while still holding the wheel. "Well?" she urged again. But my mind had gone vaporous, what I saw just shot right through any effort to contrive a meaningful pronouncement, right down to more visceral regions of response. "Well . . ." I finally muttered, "why. . . they're. . . they're most attractive."

"Yes," she countered, "but what do you think, artistically I mean?"

"Well, artistically. . .": one looking up at her on all fours —how did the photographer manage that one anyway, she must have been on a glass surface and he positioned beneath it—her legs spread and her back arched to press her thighs down at the viewer, her breasts hanging low their point of tits for touching, her higher, laughing face lion-like behind, and her black pubic middle pushing out from its forest that red, feeding interior again, like some kind of anemone, thrusting labia lips grasping for the viewer, almost squash on the lens. "Why, artistically. . . I mean. . ." I was plunging around, grabbing, but badly, for something to say (thinking *eat me, eat me*—isn't that what the pill said to Alice?—*swallow me lovely*). "I mean, they're great, you know," I finally blurted out. "They do great, how should I say . . . great justice. . . to you I mean. A real *objet d'art*. You know what I mean. . . Artful. That's what they are."

I wondered in mild disgust why I kept saying "they," as if "they" were not her. Or were they her? But artful they were, I said a mouthful of that at least.

We were at Westheimer, making a left, into the lights of late-night, honky-tonk Houston prowling up and down the avenue. I flicked off the overhead light to see better against the traffic, but kept the photos up in front of me at the wheel. I was of a mind to give them another close scrutiny, looking, I was sure, for more precise, objective things I could say in artistic judgment, rather than for just purely, I was sure, salacious motives. But she was reaching for the pictures in evident desire to have them back.

"Well, I hope they help my career. Actually, I would like to be a model."

"But you'll need clothes." No, I didn't say that, just came close. Why, after all, put clothes where nature was so utterly satisfactory without them? Or some such profound thought kept me silent.

She was tucking the pictures back in the packet. "Then you think I look pretty good in these?" she asked, and slipped the packet back in her purse.

"Oh, no question. You look really. . . most enticing. I mean, what man could look at those and not get an itch. I mean, you know what I mean."

"Well, I hope so. You know, he's a good photographer. He knew what he was doing. He understood posture. I've known him for a while, but just thought, hell, go ahead and hire him. Take a chance and see."

Well, *he* at least did some seeing. And damnit if I wasn't stuck with more than just a bit of that "itch" myself. As we headed east on Westheimer, by all the little bars and strip joints now spilling people out at the 2 o'clock closing, leaving here and there not quite sober little crowds in a glancing around of uncertainty what to do, where to go now, she crossed her legs leisurely and leaned back in the seat and yawned, stretching her khaki-sleeved arms so far back behind the seat her breasts seemed near to pop that first of the buttoned buttons. "Another long night. I'm ready for some sleep. *Ooo-aaaah.*" And her yawn cradled the whole interior of the cab in a warm, slinking drowsiness that melded with my own intense wakefulness in a drawing down to the increasing reality of that itch making itself rather too insistently known. I was fastened to the pleasure a more prostrate and indulgent reclining of myself would give me— in company of course.

Somewhere dark, in the house where she lived, of course.

For why else—my mind was bounding in stride with the throbbing and rising of that itch; against whatever enfeebled judgment I could muster it was sprinting in fact—why else would she show me those pictures? I mean, she was just more subtle than most. (Those pictures were really—I mean, it was becoming plain to me—really the utmost subtlety. This lady had style, that's all.) Why else had she shown them to me?

Westheimer had become Elgin, and we were crossing Main, approaching the Third Ward. In a couple of blocks we would turn off on her street, and, I was thinking, why not a little interim? I looked at her, now thoroughly flushed by her presence, and beginning to writhe, if pleasantly, at the stretch of my pants straight-jacketing just barely that hard thing down there, and she was smiling to herself, glowing in the dark, her perfume maddening to me, her black, curling hair, her smooth, rich neck, her large lips opened slightly and enjoying some vision in those shining eyes, all suffused it seemed with the erotic fever I had seen posed, and so artfully I was convinced now, in those publicity photos she had allowed me a glimpse.

For why else had she shown them? And as I turned off onto her street, dark and asleep in the deep night, quiet near to dream, I was almost shouting inside of me for the approaching moment when I would pull up, and I knew she would turn and look at me, all shining, and I would turn and look at her, and reach out and touch, oh yes, just the right place, and softly, within her khaki shirt, and reach over further, to those lips stretch myself, and touch, perfect, touch. . .

I stopped where she signaled, and turned to her, and I knew it was the moment, I had even forgotten there was a fare.

Her door opened for her. The tall body of the woman in a black leather, tight-fitting jump suit had simply alighted out of the dark. She towered over the cab and the petite lady hopping out to greet her, the zipper down the front of her suit pulled down low to reveal the deep cleavage in her buxom figure, her long blond hair flowing wild over her ample shoulders. "Hello, Liz," my passenger said. "God, it's good to be home, honey." Their lips met in a sensuous embrace, my passenger running her hands over the other's breasts pushing out beneath the smooth leather of her suit as they French kissed a long moment. "Here, let me pay this fellow, Liz. Hey, turn off your meter there! The fare's apt to jump another twenty cents while I'm digging in my purse. I know about that timer you guys use."

The meter off, the exact fare in my hand—and only that—then the door slammed powerfully by the blond woman in black, I just sat there stuck. I watched them walk away, the tall one's arms snug around the other's shoulders, up to the door of the house, where they stopped again to fondle and kiss each other beneath the porch light. "Come on, honey, let's go play," I heard my passenger say. "I'm needin' to unwind."

The Weed Patch

Prelude

It was dusk by the time I swung my cab into the alphabet streets of the barrio out Houston's east side, after a long trip across town bringing the tired woman home from her day's work. The streets were as tiny as their one-letter names, and sinking fast into shadow beneath the gloom of the countless trees still flourishing here even in the proximity of the port that dead-ended many of the lanes. I turned up her block, by yet another No Outlet sign, coming to a stop before a low house without a single light on, just short of a dense thicket of oaks and pecans overgrowing what was left of the broken candy-striped barrier in my headlights. From the far side of the thicket the plaintive grind of an unseen train making slow way along the waterfront heaved into the twilight a succession of low, raspy sighs, eerie and blending with the clank of metal on the rails like the final and pained exhalations of a great beast in its death rattle. It vibrated up through the pavement and pushed down through the trees, enclosed us, a tensed, unsettling sound I knew was common and hourly for this neighborhood abutting the Ship Channel.

I turned off the meter, thinking how far all this was from

the elegance and quiet, the neatly walled-in wealth of River Oaks where I had picked up my passenger. Sent off with cab fare in hand by her tall, blond mistress—who stood immaculate at the door in gown and jewels for some evening gala—the squat, middle-aged woman had said nothing after the slow, cold enunciation in careful English of her address on Ave. O, but just sat exhausted and bundled stiffly behind wary, puffy eyes in the corner of the back seat. Now she was counting out the fare from the bills given her, the train was braking in a clangor of squeals dying to a hiss, and I was studying the porch of the little house, where a row of children in tattered clothes had appeared mysteriously from the dark interior, and stood there waiting, and silent.

I didn't expect or want a tip, and gave her back the exact change. "Gracias," she said quietly, and got out of the cab. But as she was waddling toward the children, on tired feet that had probably been standing all day, a younger boy in front of the others began to cry. Didn't move, just bawled at the top of his lungs. The other children only watched. The woman now tried to run, with stumbling, awkward steps, arms outstretched and muttering a soothing of Spanish. She embraced the child, held him. But he kept crying, the others watching hollow-mouthed without emotion. The train suddenly banged and shook terribly down its length, probably picking up more cars from a side rail over in that concourse of tracks just out of sight. And I, embarrassed to witness any longer the scene on the porch—the child folded up in her arms and beginning now at least to jabber some words through his tears—made a U-turn and left.

Was the man of the house a stevedore, and working late?

Was there a man? Was there even electricity in the house, or had she defaulted on her bill? I thought of her exhaustion, the needs of those children. Hearts to assuage, mouths to feed. Their poverty, their plight, and the clank and gnash of metal filling their days, their nights. I reached 75th and turned south, wild and forlorn a moment, feeling inept, at what faced all of them I had left so easily behind on that porch.

The light-flickering towers of downtown Houston loomed straight in the new night, as I turned west on Harrisburg and tried to call my spirits back up into the heights of dreams and man-made hopes. Behind me, from the near distance, the low, breathy bellows of a ship's horn announced departure from dockside along the Channel. Going where? I wondered. Somewhere exotic, I answered, because not here, because far away. Enough, I said to myself, just get a trip and get on with it for the night. At least get back to the Westheimer district with its lights and bars and gay masquerade, its errant hedonism. Paint your night over just as that downtown paints the high stars.

But it wouldn't be Westheimer just yet. For at that moment dispatch threw Harrisburg 2 open, and I, on the sudden, was off to the Catholic Mission, just down the street.

Fugue

I arrived by the side entrance of the old, brown two-story affair, once a school, when out the near door came charging a bowlegged, glee-eyed man in baggy clothes followed swiftly by a wide-striding younger man. They bounded for the cab in a rash of croaking laughter between them. The older, baggy man was particularly bent over and looking like he had a terrible stitch in his side for all his chortling. But once tumbling into the back seat he pulled out in triumph from inside his coat a full bottle of red wine, the cork already popped and restuffed proudly.

"Ah, you got here just in time, Mister Cab Driver sir. The Father was onto us, and you know what that means. They take the bottle and kick you out for a night to think on it." He settled himself sitting forward, his head near my right shoulder, as the other slammed the door. "Out Heights way, Mister Cab Driver sir," the first continued. "We're out to the Weed Patch tonight."

"The Weed Patch?" I replied.

"Our place. I'll have you drop us off near there. It's a secret where it really is. It's our place."

The meter flag down and we were off. Cab 621 and I seemed to jump with the raw energy these two breathy characters, half huffing with impatience and half with jerky, unrestrained glee, imparted us from their head-bobbing eagerness to get on. I even squealed my tires scooting back onto Harrisburg in answer to the hurry they tumbled wacky-like at me from the back seat in a spate of in-joke laughter and elbows nudging ribs.

"That's right, Mister Cab Driver sir. Let's reel on down the road."

But the other, the younger, never spoke; he just played at shoving his older companion, emitting squeaks of pleasure as he did so that had the vocal character of a squeal-full puppy.

"That's right. That's right. The Father won't find us

tonight," the older one proclaimed.

They reeked of old clothes and scruff, a smell not too unpleasant really, but musty and sour, and panted from them in their happiness in a heavy surging at my nostrils. I leaned toward the open window just slightly to inhale the fainter pungency of city fumes, enriched by the steamy exhaust pouring from the General Foods factory we were passing, steam chutes wrapping themselves in endless curlings around the glitter of tiny lights strung everywhere like Christmas tree bulbs up the ancient smokestack structure. The place was humming in a deep power roar from behind the fluorescent glow of the opaque windows as we came to a stoplight at the far end of the building. I realized both my passengers had quieted, and were gazing in a kind of awe-struck, child-like wonder at this old but throbbing factory. They seemed in a new key of interest, and I could feel it being shifted my way as we moved on and the big head of the baggy man loomed close behind mine in the mirror. A little giggle suddenly escaped the younger one, as if he anticipated something about to transpire, something that had a decided focus, I could tell all too uncomfortably, on me.

"You know, Mister Cab Driver sir, are you. . . profound?" the big head asked me, mimicking a deep liturgical bass.

"What?" I asked.

"Are you profound?" He rounded the word to give it the utmost shape of his mouth.

"I think not," I said flatly. "Look, you guys, I don't know what you're—"

"But surely you're smart." That last word jumped from him like the crack of a whip.

"What the hell difference does it make if I'm smart?" My patience had exhausted and I just shucked it. "Look—"

"He doesn't think it makes a difference," the head in my mirror noted in a side glance at the other, who just squealed and bounced his fist in delight off the door. "He doesn't think it makes a difference. Should we tell him? Hey, what do you say we tell him."

"Tell me what?" I said, half subsiding into resignation that I best just play along.

"Why, what it means to be smart." We were approaching downtown, a sprinkling of tall lights in the Gulf sky that now argued sanity for me. Reaching high above the city floor, they seemed at least the sealed, incremental limits to some kind of purpose or achievement to climb by. Whereas I had to wonder what kind of purpose these guys I was toting in my cab could possibly realize, devoid as they were of any capacity to shift or adjust, to climb. Winos wasting themselves in the gutted vacuities of the brain. We were under a railway overpass and onto Prairie, headed into the city's heart. Just let these guys entertain themselves, I thought, and get them quickly to where they're going. So they were going to tell me about being smart, were they?

The baggy man was tapping me on the shoulder. "Mister Cab Driver sir," he said patiently, "if you think it doesn't make any difference, I must tell you: my friend here, you see, he *is* smart. He's real smart. You could hardly tell looking at him, could you? I mean, look at that grin. And he's not much for words. That's my department. But you know, Mister Cab Driver sir, he has a Ph.D.," at which, in his long enunciation of "Deeee" he made some kind of lunge against the back of my seat. The thud of it went into my back. "Do you know, Mister Cab Driver sir, what a Ph.Deeee is?"

I thought, hell, why not humor him? "Well, sir," I said, "a Ph.D., at least as I understand it, is when you're assigned to sit in a library, and you sit there, and they check to make sure you stay sitting there, and then after you have sat there for the required number of years, then they give you a Ph.D., a Philosopher Doormat for your very own porch, in honor of your patience and learned restraint and the crowds that will now come to your door to wipe their feet before your wisdom and aloof forbearance at all their dirty shoes."

"I see you're a smart ass," he said. "And I thought you was smart." But then he leaned back and gave a new elbow to his friend's ribs, who, I could see, lit up as he was by the glow of city lights filtering through the cab, rejoiced in a Buster Brown grin cut from ear to ear. He even bounced his fist off the door in a rapid staccato of approval and pleasure. "But maybe," the older man suddenly blurted out at that grin, "maybe our driver here is one of those angry young men. You suppose so? He has the long hair for it, wouldn't you say." Then, leaning forward to my shoulder again, "You must be one of those angry young men, right? But my friend," he continued, leaving me no time to reply, "my friend here, he's smart. He has a Ph.D. And do you know what his Ph.D. is in?"

"No sir," I said, feeling vaguely chastened. "I don't."

"Why, chemistry!" he shouted, with a lunge against the back of my seat that reverberated up my neck. "Do you know anything about chemistry, Mister Cab Driver sir?"

The question was more a jolt than the one he had physically delivered, a sudden thud at my being that spilled the years right out of me: high school, premed in college, the three abortive years of medical school itself that had landed me here behind the wheel of a cab, and with a sudden sadness I realized I had had no less than six full years of chemistry. And all of it wasted, it seemed. "A little, sir," I told him. "Not much though."

"Well, my friend here, he's smart. He's taught me, all about chemistry. Haven't you?" The fist banging off the door in a new round of staccato, the two fell to their bouncing gig again, bobbing jerkily their heads in arrested, held-in laughs that broke through in clucking and squeals and lots of elbows to ribs. "He's taught me," the baggy man said, resurrected at my shoulder. "You see, he's smart. And do you know, Mister Cab Driver sir, what chemistry is about? Do you?"

"No, sir. Not really," I said timidly, and apprehension gripped me as I saw that head rear high in my mirror.

"Why, molecules!" The lunge of his shout and his body this time sent me lurching, in a whip-like recoil off my seat belt so abrupt it made me grunt. We were weaving the northwest perimeter of downtown for the swing into The Heights, and I nearly slipped lanes he let me have it so hard. A fresh applause of his companion's fist staccato on the door greeted my effort to hold the cab to her lane and collect myself. "And do you know what molecules are, Mister Cab Driver sir? My friend here, you see he's taught me." A quick look back for a lane change and I saw that Buster Brown grin of the younger man beaming out the window in a kind of near-tears, eyes-closed ecstasy of jubilation. But he kept the silence.

"Well, I see you don't know, or think you don't." The big head of the older man seemed to be adjusting itself for some new pronouncement. The miasma of his odor came close, his mouth nigh to my ear, as he whispered, "But my friend here, he's smart. He's taught me." And his head rose, in a swelling at my back. I flinched, tried just to drive. "They're a kind of joining, don't you see? And do you know what they join, Mister Cab Driver sir? Do you?"

He was swelling even higher. I braced. "No," I said weakly at my mirror. "I'm not sure. What do they join?"

"Why, atoms!" I wasn't braced enough. Atoms went shattering through my body from the bang he laid this time into the back of the front seat, and this as I was just turning off Washington Ave. onto Houston Ave., going north. His bang seemed to send us pell-mell on. The road dipped immediately under a railway overpass, and I felt myself hurtling down, in trust that 621 could stay gripped to the road before this passenger flying off into his Never-Never Land of anabolic happenings, and 621 and I, all became a crazy, flying network of things, with these two winos doing the steering while they joyed in triumph at it all.

"And do you know what that means?" he shouted expansively. "Do you, Mister Cab Driver sir?" Short for words, and more than a little intimidated by this crescendo of a mad head bobbing wildly up in my mirror and carrying a football shoulder that surely blocked once for a front line, I sighed, and girded myself for whatever it was we were rising to. "Do you, Mister Cab Driver sir? I tell you, my friend here, he's smart. He's taught me. He knows. But do you?"

In a sudden interlude he sent me left. Sinister—I remem-

83

bered my Latin—sinister: left. We were now into a dark, mystery area of Houston known as The Heights. Old residences, tree-lined streets, a subsidence of aged quiet after dark—old memories finding seclusion in the pleasant decay which was peace in this introverted place. And somewhere in all these memories a Weed Patch apparently.

"You haven't answered my question, Mister Cab Driver sir," the head interrupted my thoughts, rearing like a black moon in my mirror. "About what all this means. And you know," he continued, leaning in close to my ear, "it's. . ." —and he breathed it out long and slow—"profound." It seemed to shape the whole cab into a roundness, a hugeness overarching and coming down on me, in and through me and back to him, like a spell, mad and unbeatable. Then bouncing back and giving his elbow to the younger man, whose grinning body by the door had become a sort of jello of shaking, barely constrained hysterics, though not a sound came from him now but a gurgle he couldn't quite help, the older man blurted gaily, "Why, our driver friend here, he's tongue-tied. Just to know what it means. But that's what happens to angry young men, they become tongue-tied when it really counts." And he turned back proudly, his body rising up higher than ever in my mirror. You're mad, I thought, you're absolutely mad. He seemed twice his size in the mirror, blowing up to an enormity. "So, do you know what it means?" he roared.

But he just dropped and whispered in my ear. "It's all a joining, you see, Mister Cab Driver sir. Atoms to make molecules, molecules to make bigger molecules, growing, always growing, the whole world a growing. You see, sir, chemistry is the mystery of the earth, the constant joining that is all things from the atoms they are, in order to be, in order to live. 'For to him that is joined to all the living there is hope: for a living dog is better than a dead lion.' Thus saith the preacher. And you know, son, I never had a better pulpit or congregation than this here cab to make a sermon in." He tapped me on the shoulder with his finger, while bumping his forehead lightly against my skull, then ever so casually he added, still in his throaty whisper, "Now, if you will just right politely drop us off at the next block, there, up there, we'd be much obliged."

He was full of thank you's for getting them there, his friend nodding in happy bounces of his smiling head, and I stood outside my cab—all that lunging against my body, and the jarring and intimidation and joy of these two now gone down to a whisper in me, *his* whisper—and watched them walk away, down the darkest of dark streets in a tumbled-down warehouse section of The Heights, the older man with his arm around the shoulders of the younger, the bottle in his other hand in a mild swaying as he bowlegged it in concert with his friend's taller stride. And as I watched, in my hand the three-dollar fare which they had refused to let me refuse, the two of them, in that easy rhythm of their uneven joining, were captured quietly, patiently, irrevocably by the night.

Drag

Purple	*Violet*	*Monsignor*
Fuchsia	*Lavender*	*Mulberry (Morello)*
Mauve	*Lilac*	*Mignon*
Magenta	*Plum*	

Patriarch	*Heliotrope*	*Amethyst*
Prelate	*Hollyhock*	*Amaranth*
Gridelin	*Clematis*	*American Beauty*
Bokhara	*Redgrape*	*Damson*

Jockey
Heather
Carmine (Animal Rouge)

Animal rouge. Animal rouge. Yes, the lips were like that everywhere I looked.

And everywhere I looked the ballroom was a dervish of purples I could only array in vain to the litany of an order. I had never been called here before, was only just inside the door, chanting textbook purples maybe to keep my mouth from falling entirely agape. It was a wild, gorgeous scene—

purples festooning the high walls of the club, and dependent in great folds from the ceiling, a congestion of shimmering, frenzied hangings engulfing the room, while below a buoyant and giddy legion of gowns swarmed the vast floor, pulsing and fluttering and swirling in a heat of purples flung like cool flame from the hot jazz of the speakers.

More specific. March. March.

Purple: *Imperial*
      Royal
      Roman
      Pansy
      Phlox
      Dahlia

Violet: *Parma*
      Cobalt
      Burgundy
      Hyacinth
      Hofmann's
      Petunia

Purple: *Tyrian*
      Indian
      Prune
      Raisin
      Schoenfeld's
      Auricula

But the words failed, even in battalions, to hold any beach-head for my composure, just blown to oblivion as easily as clay birds in a skeet shoot by the twin barrels of drag and hedonism letting fly in satins and silk, and scents that powered from the cloth, flooded the room. It seemed for sure that hounds released here on the trail of drag would only writhe back on themselves and gnash their own tails as prize, the escaping fox racing by them undaunted and free, the world his own, yet almost drowsy the fellow, even curling *à la mamelle* in the deep purples of the ceiling, draped buxom in their folds like swollen udders around the single galactic chandelier sparkling crystal in a thousand glittering shards of the rainbow and illuminating, if dreamily however, this heaviness of sex voyeuristically clothed and vibrant, *débauché*, to the point of sleep.

Was this sleep? A dream? I marshaled my lists yet again, in a desperate muster of mere names to resist this delirium of purple reaching a maelstrom of dance at the room's center, whirling in a mad heaven around some kind of strange, drunk requital bobbing in perfect happiness in the eye of it all I couldn't see, but beckoning me too—how could I help it?—to relent and give in and come to it too, ride wild to its heart on the eddies and flow and mating of these people. . . No, these were not people, but Bacchantes in the exile of the gods, attired for revel in every conceivable gown and swirl of exotic woman's *habit de soir*.

But these were not women.

"Cab!" I yelled over the music and my vertigo at the bartender. "Someone called." Cleopatra looked up at me from wiping the counter with a cloth of gold thread. She jangled all manner of gold bracelets and adornments, though the low cut of her lavender gown revealed inadequate use of the razor toward the cleft in her bosom. "Yes, honey," she replied in a low, sweety voice, and winked at me. Her wealth of black eyeliner tapered wonderfully from the rich impasto around the lids to a delicate, gently rising point beneath each temple, in a manner to squeeze the rather big-boned fullness of her friendly face toward at least the approximation of the gracious, long elegance of an Egyptian queen's countenance. "We can tell why you're here." (I looked down at my denim.) "Just park in front. You're the type that likes it in front anyway, aren't you?" (She winked again.) "I'll send the pair out to you in no time." I turned to go. "Oh, and honey," she continued, as I looked back from the door, "you be careful out there, you hear. They say the streets are dangerous out there. It makes you wonder why people can't learn just to have fun." She winked a third time, then turned to a tall dame (in damson?) stepping up to request a beer.

Back out the door the black swath of Travis Street was a relief. Dangerous or not, it was asphalt, hard sidewalks, reality. Under the streetlamps grey pools of light illumined weakly the late night, and the air was the malodor of refinery fumes drifting west in the dank, heavy atmosphere. Reality. I breathed it in full, and admired the scurry of a rat along the electrical line overhead. His instinct and precision in perfect habitat in this midnight silence he ruled, perfect pace, as he sprinted the length of the block in seconds and vanished utterly into his domain. King Rat. I tendered my allegiance, in a pact sealed by the sense of things defined and in a straight trajectory that he mapped upon the void.

For I felt in my domain too, defined and with a trajectory too, even enjoyed the clack of my shoes on the surface of the sidewalk as I returned to my cab, enjoyed the clean slam of the door, and the confident revs of the engine as I started it up and moved 621 forward along the curb until opposite the door of the club. Everything clear and hard-edged again, straight.

The door opened in moments, and out came a bulky figure in purple gown moving quickly to the cab. But lo and behold, the light that blinded Saul with the roar of *Quo vadis?* could not have been a more sudden surprise than the vision that now dazzled and confounded me in her wake: a tall, coiffured beauty in a bustier of radiant, *white* silk standing resplendent and divine in the doorway. Where had she been in all that swarm of purple? Pure grace was the sheen of her décolletage, hugging pertly the curves of her bosom, and her low back revealed teasingly behind a waist-long tumble of black hair as she turned to have a last word with someone in the club. She wore chic, elbow-length white gloves, highlighting the nude allure of her shoulders, and pearl earrings that glinted with just the tiniest cut of a diamond each in a pleasantly subtle downplay of the spangles that danced from the little gold purse she carried. But nothing in her adornment could rival the shimmering, sheer white of her dress, a radiance pure Renaissance, married at her hips to the slenderest, perfect curvature of her body tapering snugly down her length to the lustrous *punkt* of a pair of gold high heel shoes.

Queen Bee. Where had you been in all that swarm of purple? Baffled, I could only think her the conjury of some strange metamorphosis, magic as foam-risen Venus delivered whole from the sea. Born at that door as if from a chrysalis.

Her purple companion had long since entered the back seat of the cab and slid across, announcing in a gruff, accented voice an address on Ave. K, in the barrio east of downtown. Queen Bee now approached across the walk as I watched, her long hair swishing lazily across her back from the neat coiffure bound near the top in a bright gold band, and slipped into the back with an easy swing of her body, rushing perfume ahead of her in a flush of delicate musk that wrapped round me from behind and stopped me right there in sudden, erotic arrest.

The back door closed with a light click. "Okay, we go now. Let's go," the purple one pressed impatiently. But I was unable, simply staring in my mirror at her olive-complexioned face who sat behind me, inundating me with a strange import of déjà vu and famishment from the nature of the perfume she wore. I knew it somewhere. My fingers just walked around the wheel in my captivated state.

"We go. We go."

"Yes, yes, of course," I finally muttered, and fumbled for the hard edge of the meter flag. Pleased at least to have an excuse to look back in order to slip into the one-way stream of Travis—though devoid of any traffic at this hour—I unhappily caught a good look at the big face of my purple passenger. She hadn't shaved nearly recent enough; I was appalled to see black stubble over her swarthy jaws, and her coiffure a mess of mangy ends sticking out this way and that. But peripherally I saw the beauty, gazing rapt at her consort in a mild, high bearing of her regal face that jarred and discomposed me in a rant of wrong, this is all wrong. She's not . . . How can she be?

I was driving north, and the one in purple was talking, in Spanish, which I couldn't understand, a manic, gravelly, haughty voice that seemed more appropriate for Pancho Villa or one of his *guerrilleros* boasting of victory than in a love journey home in the company of this queen who sat beside her.

She hadn't spoken. Was she. . . ? I kept asking myself. But how could she be?

She was a woman, I kept answering myself. She was a woman. And this was some kind of travesty, a mistake.

If not agitated enough, I was a complete prisoner of her perfume, gliding into my nostrils and soaking me with something I couldn't name, couldn't reach, teasing me, till the need was almost unbearable to just turn around, seize her bare shoulders and shout please, please, into that depth of her person so quiet, ineluctable, back there. Crazy, I gripped the wheel till my hands went sore.

You could even touch her, caress her, if. . .

That damn purple brute. She kept talking. Go back to Pancho Villa, why don't you, and the mountains and dust. Then suddenly I saw in my mirror that brute reach her hands across in a most unseemly and forward manner to feel up this prize she had no right to claim.

Only then did my white beauty speak. Almost in a whisper, mind you, but in her gentle Spanish it was clear she was protesting, trying to fend off the other. But not even her soft, pleading, tender tones could hide the suddenly brutal fact (for me) that she too (damn) was as drag as the other.

The fox, fie on him! The voice had at some time broken in the past, and not even hormones, and all else that was perfect and graceful, alluring about her (those breasts? those hips? angel white at the door) could (damn, damn) deceive me longer.

Riling with rebuke, almost to tears with stupidity, I cursed my foolery in the name of His Highness, King Rat I'd seen, ruler alike of electrical lines and the fouled hopes of human folly. And renewed my fealty with a burst of speed and sarcasm that sent cab No. 621 hurtling through the lights on the straight trajectory of just another trip, precise and fast, to make a few bucks at the end and be on to the next one.

But damn them both, the scenario in the back seat worsened—I couldn't drive fast enough. She was crying out against the other, her perfume overwhelming me with something I couldn't name, compelling me with the need I do something for her. And suddenly my repugnance was gnashing its own tail, desperate to help her but stupid, the compulsion becoming crazy again to turn and grab her bare shoulders behind me, shout please, please, from the crazy, wild indecision I was deep into the apparition maybe she was, all memory and familiar someway, inundating me like this with that perfume I couldn't name, a memory I couldn't grasp.

Her hairy mate pushed and probed relentlessly in the darkness back there, even giggled several times. Her voice in white rose in desperate appeal, carried now on the waves of her perfume insistent and deep to the heart of something I was, an apparition maybe I was, and suddenly it happened, crossing the empty streets of downtown, it came crying out of me: *Écusson* , the Shield, that was it, calling from a girl redolent with that perfume I had loved once, from the depths of a time wonderful and lost I had known once, from New Haven, Conn., Macy's where I'd found it, a timid first time at a perfume counter, and the Park Plaza Hotel where we'd christened it, in my first surrender, wild from a time young and lost that was suddenly remembered now. A past I'd forsaken, had failed, in a fresh rebuke that came up to slap me at this moment. And reeling from that memory something came clear to me: it was not that she was a man or a woman behind me, but someone beautiful and vulnerable, like the girl odorous of the same perfume I had known and loved before her, calling out to all of us in fealty to the King to renounce him, let the rat clatter into the trash heaps, be instead the keeper of the grail, the chalice, what it was she was holding out to me right now, if only we'd take it and say yes, yes, yes to what she was behind me, and now cried out for me to defend.

Purple, Fuchsia, Mauve, Magenta. . . I was freed like a butterfly from the capture of my confusion. My anger came free as well, she suddenly screamed in a frenzy behind me and I rammed to the curb and yelled, "Stop! Stop it right now! Leave her alone!" staring brutally over my shoulder at the purple aggressor. Sheepishly she sat up, and slid back to her side of the seat.

I drove on, in the sudden silence of the cab lifted and free, fluttering like the butterfly I felt, in gay counterpoint to the high, solid towers of downtown Houston we passed— modeled powerfully at their base by the streetlamps and shadows of an empty city, in homage to the base of power they were for legions of executives now asleep at home. But I was not asleep, and my wings brushed stars the heights of which Shell One and the Exxon Building couldn't dream of reaching, in a tapestry of the air flooded in *Écusson* and possibilities, weaving me more and more into her who sat right behind me, ineluctable, real, and yes a woman.

The fox had found me. I was real. We were running together, through the fields, loose, wonderful, randy, *purple, fuchsia, mauve, magenta*, drowned to excess in purples and perfume as finally, a free man, I touched her running beside me, her shoulders, and said please, please, I love you maybe . . . I. . .

Damnit, one learns things.

Pancho Villa had paid me, grinning not so sheepishly now, and forced her way out of her side first, then her slow, graceful companion following in a slide across the back seat that rippled the air with soft sound of her silk and body, perfume to make me dizzy, to make me ache for her, who would not be mine after all. My hands gripped the wheel, I could think of nothing to say, only watch, as she swished up from the seat and stepped into the night. The other had already opened the front door of the little house, nestled behind a large white oak tree, and gone inside.

She closed the door of the cab with a light shove, and I watched her walk away, white silk whispering snug from her body, and her long black hair bobbing lightly upon her bare back, under that enormous tree and up to the porch. Then it was she turned and looked at me, silhouetted in chiaroscuro beneath a small lamp above the door, and I looked at her, and for a moment we were complete that way, for a long moment, before she turned and entered the house, closing the door behind her.

Exile of the gods. It recurred to me. And Cleopatra speaking to me over a bar rag of gold thread. The Bacchantes dancing through their mythic fields, the chalice still there for the offering. It seemed all true, as I lingered before that closed white door beneath its little lamp, the single light casting up into the night strange yet breathing shadows upon the overarching limbs of the great oak above. Her image still there, profound and quiet before her portal.

The goddess. Looking at me. And, incredibly, a man. I had seen her in a man.

I drove away, newly exiled myself, into the byways of the night. Dreaming, aroused, loose in the fields. Joining the fox.

Justice

The announcement came over dispatch as I waited second in line at Westheimer One. "Attention all drivers. We have a pirated vehicle. Be on the lookout for Yellow Cab 414. Sometime over ten minutes ago 414 was seized by passengers believed to be Greek sailors. The driver reports he picked them up on Telephone Road near Griggs, and that they forced him from his vehicle while he was northbound on Wayside, in the vicinity of Lawndale. They then made a U and headed south on Wayside. We presume they are trying to return to their ship, though they failed to tell the driver exactly which ship or which dock was their destination, and evidence is they don't know where they're going. Please be advised, the police have out an all-points. If you sight 414 notify us immediately for relay to HPD. Do not try to interfere, just notify us. I repeat. . ."

"Oh boy, did you hear that?" It was Bill the Greek, hopping out of the cab in front of me. He was a tall, talkative young man whose family owned a fashionable Greek restaurant over on Shepherd. But tired of waiting tables for his uncle he had taken up the wheel of a cab about the time I did. "Fellow countrymen no less," he shouted again at me, arms spread wide in excitement, like he wanted to take flight off his toes. "Damnit, Moo, if we don't need *something* to happen around here." He came running back to my window. "Hell, I think I'll go look for 414. I'm not making any money tonight, anyway. Are you?" He peered in at me, sweat bouncing off his forehead from the warm, moist, still night it was.

"No, not actually, Bill. Just a few trips so far. It's damn slow, for sure."

"Well, I bet those Greek pirates aren't being slow. I wonder if they have any idea where they're going. South on Wayside makes you wonder. Look, I need a little adventure. You go ahead and take first in line. Maybe that'll pick things up for you. I'm off looking for countrymen. Nothing better to pick things up for me."

"Bill, this is a big city. You can't hope to find them. If they don't know where they're going they could end up anywhere. Besides, wherever it is the police will be there first."

"Moo, you can be a letdown, you know that? What, is adventure dead around here? Look, I have a nose for Greeks you wouldn't believe. You're too American to know anything about racial consciousness, but we Greeks are cast in a way to draw to one another. And in a big foreign city like this the pull is even greater. We come in like in a net. You Americans are simply too foreign to one another to understand any of this. I'll find them, don't you worry."

"What do you suppose they stole the cab for?" I was trying to slow Bill down. Sometimes he needed slowing down.

"It's obvious. They spent all their money in the bars along Telephone. You know we Greeks are big spenders, but we're a practical people. How else were those guys going to get back to their ship, which is probably leaving tonight, than by commandeering a cab? Hey, it makes sense." He seemed positively proud, pressing his head near mine. His black hair was beginning to stick out the way we were used to when he succumbed to one of his expansive moods.

"Well, I hope the driver's okay. I don't know who drives 414."

"I don't either. But don't worry. He'll have something to tell his grandchildren someday." Two months of cab stand conversations with Bill had revealed him an inveterate romantic. Not even a University of Houston education had mellowed his temperament. It had sent him out with a B.A. in History (not a degree in Business, to the immense dissatisfaction of his uncle apparently), which was good for waiting tables, not commanding a deck under the black flag. But he belonged in the swashbuckling era, with loose blouse and red sash, a great sword in his hand, giving orders in pursuit of a Spanish galleon. "Besides, Moo, there is always justice to these things," Bill added. "If anyone knows about justice we Greeks do. Didn't we teach it to the world?"

"Well, I'm sure the driver is demanding justice right now," I said easily, trying to humor my manic friend.

"Oh, he'll get it one way or another, believe me. Dominoes keep falling, that's what keeps this world tight and wild. In this case I just want to be part of it, is all. So I'm off." He banged his palm on the sill of my window, and turned for his cab.

"Westheimer One. Westheimer One." It was dispatch, calling the lead car on our stand.

"Hold on, Bill," I said. "This is for you, friend." I held the mike out to him as far as the cord would allow. "Hurry up, he'll throw it open any moment."

He was stopped in his tracks, hesitating. "Damn you, Moo." He wheeled and grabbed the mike, springing the cord right into my face he pulled on it so hard. "396," he barked.

"396," dispatch replied. "Art Wren's. The Silver Dollar."

"The Silver Dollar," Bill sighed into the mike, acknowledging the trip. Then he thrust the mike back at me. "Damn you, Moo. Why didn't you answer it? I gave you the front of the line."

"Because you need the money, spending it on books the way you do. And you're practical. You know, 'We Greeks are spenders, but we're a practical people.' I quote a reliable source."

"Yeah, and there's such a thing as being *too* practical. But you're too American to understand the distinction. The Silver Dollar," he wailed. "It's probably one of the little darlin's only wants to go a few blocks."

"Probably is, Art Wren's and all. But that'll leave you time to go find your countrymen *and all* afterwards." I laughed, I couldn't help it. Bill was incredible to think he could find 414 in a city the size of Houston. Sometimes he was just too much. And if it hadn't been for his peroration on all this outside my cab, which was so like him, he would already have been halfway to wherever it was he would fail to find them and never been caught by dispatch in the first place. But Bill *was* Greek in one way: he had to nail everything down with talk before embarking on anything. He seemed to believe that it was words which drove things into reality. Really, he was too much.

"And you bet I'll find them," he said, stomping off to his cab. Then, before getting in, he turned to me. "Long live pirates!" he shouted. "Remember, we Greeks were first the infamous 'sea people'." The door slammed, and 396 pulled away, squealing tires as it jumped into Montrose and was gone.

I eased forward to the front position, thinking how funny it was Bill spoke of his "countrymen" and "you Americans," calling Houston "a big foreign city." For he was as American as I was, Houston-born in fact. But there was something, I couldn't really deny it, that cleaved to the Old World about him, something beneath that manic, ingenuous American exterior of his and that playing Hollywood with his heritage which entertained us. I had often had some vague sense of it, like an engine driving him from deep, that refused to believe the world was all so exterior and manageable as we made it out to be in this country, but that it had deep rules about it we tended to lose sight of in our polyglot, everyone-for-himself world of upward mobility. "There is always justice to these things," he had said. "That's what keeps this world tight and wild." Maybe some of this had to do with the deep injustice he had admitted to me his extended family felt, that he gave up helping the family business to do something for himself, be a loner. Had never even gotten the right kind of education when they gave him the chance in the first place, but been a loner all the way for something impractical in their opinion. "Dominoes keep falling." How could anyone be a loner in a world like that? Really, Bill did walk a tightrope somewhere in that mind of his. I sat, waiting for dispatch, thinking of these things.

Afterwards, on returning to the lot at 5 in the morning, I would hear of the young black driver forced by the Greeks from his cab, seeking help and a phone in a nearby apartment complex that was locked up with gates, and being discovered wandering around the back of the building by the white security guard, who mistook him for a burglar and bashed him hard over the head with a truncheon. Pleas from the stricken, bleeding man would finally lead to a phone call to Yellow Cab Co. and vindication of his story. I learned he was a new driver, had just started a few days back. A loner, who had just moved to this city, and was part-timing at night to augment a warehouse job during the day.

Maybe the incredible is just a step away if you believe in it. Or if someone else does who is pulling you with them. I had waited at the stand only a few minutes when dispatch called Westheimer One. I was given a trip to the phone company at Elgin and Main, where I picked up a young black man dressed crisply in shirt and tie. He had been working late at his desk, and was now headed home to an address in the Third Ward. As we approached this sprawling black ghetto word came over dispatch that cab 414 had been sighted northbound on Dowling Street, headed at high speed right into the heart of the Third Ward. "Oh boy," I thought, echoing Bill, and quickly told my passenger the story of the stolen cab. "Those honkies must really be lost," he said with a wry chuckle. "No docks in this part of town, just black folk. Those Greeks just found Africa. The night must be getting blacker and blacker everywhere they look."

"The wrong way for the Enlightenment, hey?" I said, feeling some rising manic mood in myself that was strange, but delightful.

"It was always honkies thought the Enlightenment was white," my passenger grinned rather coldly, his white teeth prominent behind his curled-back lips in the black of that very black face. "There'll sure be enlightenment if they hit somebody."

That silenced me on the spot, but I picked up speed for the corner of Dowling and Elgin, feeling suddenly the coincidence of all this as an irresistible drawstring tugging me into whatever heart of things it had encompassed. "Oh boy" kept bounding from my brain, like a wild Bill of a Greek whose lasso it was had me in its pull, and now the whole ward it seemed, as sirens erupted in a wide, encircling stridency echoing through the streets, and suddenly Hieronymus Bosch returned to Houston could not have pictured things more strangely.

The crowd ahead swelled from all directions, like waves of a black ocean that had finally found a dock here in the Third Ward to crash against. But it all stopped, oddly stilled at the center, where police cars strobed their lights in lurid dreaminess over the amazed melee of blacks surrounding the scene at Dowling and Elgin, catty-corner from Emancipation Park. We had to stop, as the crowd had closed off the street. Jumping out, my passenger and I peered over shoulders, even as people peered oddly back at my yellow cab and some of them pointed at her in hushed undertones of some untoward recognition that made me just a little jittery. But gaining a vantage point the reason was made clear, for my cab's yellow sister was the attraction at the very center of all this commotion, in the embrace of a lamppost beaming down a white arc of consternation on the crumpled front end where 414 had jumped the curb and come to an abrupt, ramrod of a stop. All four doors were open, and from the interior police were quietly handcuffing and removing a small cadre of very white, very terrified-looking men, who hung close to their captors and only too willingly slipped into the back seat of the police cars awaiting them.

Some group started to sing over to the side, women mainly, swinging their hips and languid limbs African-like, and clapping their hands to the beat, a Greek chorus maybe, intoning the fate of the heroes. But others were laughing now, many were pointing in playful commentary with their neighbors, the mood of this crowd certainly upbeat and festive.

But the play wasn't over. For suddenly bursting up Dowling Street, horn blaring and scattering hundreds, roaring right into the center and skidding to a stop in a great squeal of rubber beside 414, came none other than cab 396.

"Damnit Bill, what are you doing?" I said aloud, trying to push forward but unable to. And out he jumped, spreading wide his arms in excitement, like he wanted to take flight off his toes, and shouted at the police cars loading up their prisoners, "*Zeto e pirates!*"

At our next meeting Bill would explain he had shouted the Greek for "Long live pirates!" Of course he was escorted immediately to his cab by the police and the crowd pushing in to know who he was, or what, in all this. The place was restored in remarkably good time, however, because the crowd remained in a good mood. Entertainment like this didn't come often to the Third Ward. But it did take a while, after the prisoners were driven away, and 396 was accompanied by another patrol car from the premises, to clear everyone away from 414. The banged-up front end where the cab had said hello to the lamppost evoked curious wonder and much pantomime and talk and "Whoooee. Those honkies didn't know where they was at. Oh man, the night must have seemed some black man to them. Runnin' scared into the heart of the black night."

Later I would learn the police didn't book them, but returned them immediately to their ship, which sailed the next morning. 414 was towed away, Bill was long since elsewhere in the city, my passenger was at home, and I drove back through here, by pockets of people who lingered in conversation, and still I did not know of the young black driver who was now at Ben Taub Hospital being treated for severe wounds to the head, a possible fracture of the skull.

Later still, two weeks in fact, Bill was called from the lead position at Westheimer One to pick up a passenger on Alabama. We would be told over dispatch to be on the lookout for a young, fashionably dressed black woman who fled the cab immediately and disappeared utterly into the black night.

She was never found.

Bill was rushed to Ben Taub by ambulance with a bullet

in his back. She had sat behind him, and they hadn't gone two blocks when she fired.

We never knew who she was, or if Bill had been in a manic mood and opened his mouth in some wrong way. He always liked to talk to his passengers.

Weeks later he was out of the hospital, able to function. She had missed his spine. Last I heard he was back again waiting tables for his uncle, over on Shepherd.

Mockingbird

I picked him up at The Silver Dollar on Westheimer. The former Art Wren's had become a hangout for the gay crowd, which always packed into the place after the 2 AM closing of the bars. But this passenger was different; just a kid to start with. And he was easy enough to spot through the cafe's big plate glass window as I pulled up: small, sitting alone at a table by the door, yet his legs crossed and elbow cocked back over his chair as he gazed out the window, his chin held high, in a decided attitude of detached hauteur, even defiance, against the backdrop of the cafe's usual bedlam of aggressive males posturing in tight jeans and cut-off sleeves, a drunken swirl of pushy seduction and pairing off that loudly occupied the premises behind him.

He came bounding out to the street the moment I stopped, and hopped in the front seat. "Are you the one who called?" I asked him.

"I just stopped in there to use the phone. But what a zoo. Creeps and fags all over the place. You'd think they had something better to do than crawl all over one another. Jesus, they feel each other up in public in there."

"Where to?"

"Out Clinton Drive. Galena Park, just off the Channel. I'll show you."

The meter flag over, I swung into a U-turn and headed east on Westheimer.

I estimated his age at maybe sixteen. Short blond hair, creamy skin, real clean-cut looking in turquoise knit shirt over slacks of the same color. But nervous, not able to sit still. Even though he draped his left arm over the seat between us in an effort to appear relaxed, his chin high in that haughty pose I had seen through the window, he was so short of stature it was actually awkward for him, and he couldn't keep it up for long. He leaned forward, elbows on his knees and rubbing his hands together, then leaned back again, fidgeted. He couldn't find the right position.

"Jesus, creeps and fags everywhere in this part of town. The whole place is going to shit."

"What's a kid like you roaming around these parts at 3 AM anyway?" I thought to engage him in some conversation, maybe settle him down. We had a distance to go.

"Watch who you call a kid, buddy. I know the streets of this town better than you will in ten years of driving a cab."

"Do you live in Galena Park?"

"Look, I live everywhere. Does that answer your question, mister? But I grew up off the Channel, sure."

"That's a pretty rough part of town."

"No rougher than any other. That's if you know your way around. I was living in and out of bars and talking up sailors and cowboys when I was just knee-high. I know the scene."

"Do you go to school?"

"School? Sheeit. Who you kidding, mister? School is

making a buck and feeding myself. School is the two hundred dollars I made tonight rolling some old jerk. He's probably waking up right now with a sore head, wondering what hit him. Teach him to be nice to strangers."

"I see."

I was making good time through the empty streets, and turned northeast, up the lonely blocks along the edge of the city's Third Ward. The towers of downtown Houston became visible off to the left, a sprinkling of faint lights suspended in the opacity of a fine mist, like a nebula of stars in the Gulf sky. The hegemony of business and power embodied in those tall buildings seemed to be floating free of any foundation, a thing of celestial simplicity and remoteness all the more apparent in contrast to the hard reality of these streets through which I drove and their dreary emptiness at this hour.

"At least you seem to know where you're going," my passenger said. "So many cabbies are fuckin' imbeciles and you have to tell them every turn."

"Well, so far, so good. I can get us to Clinton. But after that I'm just another imbecile. The Channel always confuses me. It's just a tangle of darkness and dead-end streets and locked gates, refineries and factories that are their own world, keeping the rest of us out. I often think of the port as like a jungle, and the Channel a great snake hidden in there, twisting through it all yet damn hard to find."

"Well, you got the jungle part right. You're talking about my backyard, mister."

"Did you ever think of going to sea?"

"Didn't have to. The sea came to me. Listen, I've rolled

111

more sailors than you could believe. Was part of an operation I finally took over. Our sole occupation and income were the drunk sailors stumbling out of bars. They wouldn't know where they was at, and we'd oblige them with directions. They always ended up behind the bushes, with a sore head and empty wallet. Of course, they had to hope their wallet wasn't empty already by the time we got to them. Man, they were doomed sons of bitches if we found they were broke.

"I tell you the easiest guys are the Russians," he continued. "They're so unsure of themselves, and they really think Americans are nice people. Well, I've taught a few of them, I tell you. Done my part for the Cold War, left a bunch of them cold. I remember reading in the paper about two of them we'd rolled and left near dead at the back of a lot. The police found them and got them to a hospital, where they started howling and screaming about an 'official' protest. 'Official', my ass. Boy, they were a couple of dumb Russkies. I just wanted to say, 'Hey, welcome to America, boys. Land of the free. Home of the brave.' And all that good shit."

"How free are *you*, may I ask?"

"Free enough to keep anyone from fucking with me. Life don't come freer than that, mister."

"Were you ever caught, doing all this?"

"You were talking about the snake, remember? Well, I *am* the snake. Growing up the way I have you learn how to disappear. Be there, but not be there. But, sure, I've done some time, in juvenile. Once got turned in by a 'friend'. He found out what a friend I could be when I got out."

I decided not to ask how.

But I noticed my passenger had relaxed a little. Talking

seemed to have mollified that nervous, jittery air of his. He didn't fidget so much, but sat more consistently hunched forward, elbows on his knees and hands together, just barely able to see over the dashboard. I wondered in fact what he did see when he looked down the road of his life.

And it amazed me not a little to think that in slightly different circumstances I might have been one of his victims. Maybe rolled as easily as those sailors, as unsuspecting as they of that clean-cut innocence I imagined he could play to the hilt. That small frame, almost baby face. He must have been a master of technique, a lightning when he struck and brought someone down. I saw no reason to doubt it. I glanced at my purse, on the seat right beside me, atop the trip sheet. But he had made his money tonight; I was probably safe.

We were up the east side of downtown, approaching Navigation. "Do you usually work the Westheimer district," he asked, "or was it just an accident you were over there tonight?"

"No, no accident. Westheimer is my base."

"How can you stand it over there, all those creeps and fags everywhere?"

"They're as good passengers as anyone. And they give me steady work between midnight and five. It's fine as long as they don't grab at you while you're trying to get them to where they're going. I draw the line there."

"Hell, mister, I'd draw the line sooner'n that. I'm going to kill one someday, I swear."

"Certainly I don't have to remind you that the bars in your part of town have the worst reputation in Houston. The gays are not a violent group, except maybe with each other in private sometimes. And many a love nest has that problem, anyway. But you read about killings all the time over where you're going."

"Just stupid-ass cowboys, is all. Most of them urban cowboys, who don't know what to do with themselves—you know, no more frontier for them to get lost in, keep them out on the prairie at night singing 'Get Along, Little Dogie' and all. So they tote guns and pride in the city, looking for trouble. And find it."

"Well, what's so much better about 'stupid-ass cowboys' than the gay crowd? The gays aren't looking for trouble, just love. If they do it a different way from the rest of us that's their business."

He looked abruptly at me with an odd expression on his face, his head drawn back slightly, his brow furrowed. For the first time a hint of fear and anguish startled his eyes. He seemed suddenly very small, staring strangely at me that way, fragile even, with that short blond hair dropping in a little bang across his forehead, and that small, intense face, and that hunched-over posture with his hands together, all giving the momentary impression of hurt innocence rather than hard experience.

"Because 'stupid-ass cowboys' are at least afraid," he finally said, turning from me to look ahead again. "At least that's honest, mister, to be afraid. And they've got pride, real pride; they're trying to stand up for something. The world just doesn't let 'em, is all. Got 'em locked up, all of us. Hell, I've seen a fair few of them shot in bars, you don't have to tell me. And their pride all went up in smoke, for sure. Just 'stupid-ass', for sure."

"But what kind of pride can there possibly be in a bar brawl?"

"Boy, I really have a talker in you, don't I. Think you're real smart, don't you, and know which end is up."

"All I know is the 'up' end is usually down." I didn't mean that to come out the way it did. I looked at my passenger, afraid I'd insulted him. But he was just looking back at me askance, puzzlement on his face, as if he was trying to read me, not counterattack.

"Sheeit," he finally said, shaking his head and looking away. "Down, up, who the hell cares."

I made Navigation and headed east. With downtown behind us the city seemed drearier than ever. The mist that hung over us blotted out the stars, so the sky was black. Under the occasional bare bulb highlighting a sign, the only language through here was Spanish.

"Beanerville," my passenger muttered. "Man, the Beaners have taken over this part of town. You know, mister, what is it about this city? Every damn city I guess. Everybody's got to mark off their turf, you know what I mean? Got to have their cage. If it's not the fags and Westheimer, it's the Beaners and their barrio; if it's not the Beaners, it's the niggers and their wards. And if it's not them it's white trash everywhere else. Garbage loads of that, flyin' their red, white, and blue proud as can be every Fourth and Memorial Day, and saying 'keep out' to everybody else. I mean, what kind of place is America anyway? The only America I've ever known is just a damn zoo."

"But that's the American dream, isn't it?" I said, shrugging with a chuckle. "Everyone trying to find their place, their cage?" But my humor was artificial. Something in this boy's anger was contagious, and depressing. Real.

"Shit, it's not a dream, it's a nightmare. That's why I like 'stupid-ass cowboys', mister. Because you look at 'em, and they're still trying to live a dream. They still want to have space, freedom, to fight for. And all they can do is get shot in a bar," he said, wagging his head in disgust. "Or maybe go to 'Nam and get shot in the jungle by gooks. It's a stupid-ass world, for sure. Doesn't have anything to fight for anymore but the wrong thing."

"You don't think there's a right thing anymore?"

"Hell no. Except taking care of yourself. Yourself is the only one. The world's shit, you know that, mister? Shit."

We had reached the industrial sector of Navigation, of dark warehouses mainly, and I pushed on, wondering who this boy's parents were, or had been. My passenger had become restive again, rubbing his hands together almost violently, then gripping them hard, in alternate sequence, all the time looking down at the floor and frequently shaking his head. At one point his whole body seemed to shudder.

I reached 69th Street and turned north. We were up the viaduct over the Buffalo Bayou, and to the right, in the Turning Basin around a bend in the bayou, appeared the superstructure of a large ship being maneuvered around by unseen tugs in a swath of light and the roaring of machinery that announced the beginning of the Channel. "Well, there's someone with somewhere to go," I said. "That ship could be headed anywhere, Corpus Christi down the coast, or maybe Singapore. There are still places to go in this world. Maybe you should think of going to sea."

"No," he said. "There's only one place I want to go, and that's where we're going right now. Jesus, I need a hit bad."

"Oh. Is that where we're going?"

"Damn right that's where we're going. Why do you think I needed that two hundred? The stuff's expensive, you know. The only reason I'd be over where you found me. The dealer's off Westheimer, another fag like the rest."

At the north end of the viaduct I looped down to Clinton Drive and headed east. To our right railroad tracks cluttered the roadside with tank cars and other freight, beyond which grain elevators and warehouses and plants of one kind or another lined the near side of the Channel in a chiaroscuro of bright lights and darkness charged with unseen activity and purpose, but thwarting any view at all of the ships and the piers at the threshold of all that activity still further beyond. Then willowy trees in a dense row appeared along the roadside, leaning their tenebrous limbs into my headlights and blocking a view of even the railway tracks, as if pushing us further back from any glimpse of the port. It was a feeling I had had before, of the Port of Houston being a zone for only the initiate, the rest of us excluded, in the loneliness of just passing by.

My passenger was looking at the trees. "You know how many times I've slept beneath those trees there? And in the spring they're full of mockingbirds. Between the tracks and the road, a mockingbird's kingdom." He continued looking at the trees, as if in a reverie. "You know, mister," he finally resumed, "it's funny maybe, but I love listening to mockingbirds. It's when I no longer stop to listen to them jamming away on every other bird's tune, when I hear them but don't, that I know it's time. I need a hit, and bad. After that, mockingbirds just light up my mind. I can listen to them for hours. And now that they're nesting again, it's a real concert. There's one mocker in particular, he lives in a tree out back of where we're going, and he just starts up and sings any time of the night. Fills the whole place with sound. Bet you in fact he's singing when we get there. Just bet you."

"Well, I'm in agreement with you there. I've always had a fondness for the mocker myself."

"You know, they're worth the whole damn human race. They just seem to enjoy life. It's amazing. They set up shop anywhere in the city, doesn't matter how crowded or ugly, or if there's some big machine roaring away next door, or trucks and noise. Just give them a tree or a bush, is all. If it weren't for mockingbirds I sometimes think I'd go crazy. As a kid, sleeping on the street more often than not, I'd listen to them. Mocking the hell out of every other bird and having a ball. Have you ever seen them attack a cat?"

"They go for the eyes, don't they?"

"Sure do. They band together and go right for that cat." And he imitated a dive bomber with his right hand, swooping down for the kill. "I love that flash of white from their wings when they're fightin' mad and diving at that cat. He better get lost, and fast, or he's one blind puss."

We passed the Athens Bar & Grill, all shuttered up now. Except for the odd truck now and then, or a semi, we had Clinton all to ourselves. Then there was the occasional shadow walking along the edge of the road, beneath those trees.

"It's not far now. Almost there," he said, still leaning forward, elbows on knees, his eyes just barely able to see over the dashboard.

Moments later we entered Galena Park, a small island of a town surrounded by vast tracts of industrial zoning, and he directed me to the right, down a lone residential street in the direction of the Channel. The houses we passed were all small, dilapidated and dark on cinder blocks, and what streetlamps there were spaced well apart, creating tiny patches of bare, empty light on the uneven asphalt. In the penumbra of one such lamp I saw the carcass of an air-conditioning unit fallen into the weeds right below the boarded-up window it had once occupied. The car jounced through a succession of unrepaired potholes.

Just short of some railroad tracks he told me to pull up. I stopped, in front of a little white frame house on the right that seemed sagging into thick grass. Well behind it a white garage apartment was faintly visible in among a grove of trees. There was not a single light from either structure to suggest a sign of life, only the white paint to assert itself against the darkness. But on down the road about half a mile the lights of a grain elevator defined its bulk against the moist night, and much further away, off to the left, the calligraphy of lights strung up and down the towers and vents of a refinery on the far side of the Channel were enmeshed and diffused by the mist in a manner to suggest a galaxy seen through nearer stars. Suddenly, sitting there behind the wheel and looking, I was hit by a sense of conjunction, a rush upon my veins, as if the night from this very spot reached out to matters of great importance, timeless patterns of some enormous destiny poised here in those lights across the void, the space and bigness of it all. Mystery danced upon my body in a shiver of goosebumps.

"It's a fine little corner I have, isn't it, mister?" He was counting out the fare.

"Yes, yes," I was muttering, still entranced by whatever it was had a hold of me in this darkest of places.

He paid me, adding two dollars tip, and got out of the cab. "Thanks for the trip," he said, and was moving away when suddenly he turned back. "Listen!" He leaned in at the open window, but cocked his ear to something he heard. "Turn off your engine, and listen!"

I did what he asked. And sure enough, through the misty, vast air of the silent night, a single mockingbird could be heard from out back by that garage apartment.

"He knows where it's at," the young man said, slapping his hand on the sill of the window. "Now I'm going to join him. Once again, thanks for the trip, mister."

Then he walked away, quickly disappearing behind the white frame house.

I sat, listening. The mockingbird was trumpeting up a storm of imitation back somewhere in the black of that place. Claiming a tree for his own. In defense of his nest, his own.

Dark Side of the Moon

I picked him up at a gas station where Old Spanish Trail merged with South Main, just north of the Astrodome. The Dome was dark, the Astros out of town, the 8th Wonder of the World imparting a huge sense of eerie absence to the night. The honky-tonk and bright neon of South Main seemed a feeble gesture in comparison, the entanglement of lights a mere scrawl of calligraphy at the foot of the giant shadow sweeping its black sphere of a roof in a massive arc of dominance and void as simple and austere as the dark side of the moon come to rest here among us.

My passenger emerged from under the bright fluorescence of the station. He was a tall, neatly dressed man in his fifties, sporting a white shirt and crimson tie over dark slacks, and walking deliberately up to the cab with an almost over-broadcast air of serious intent in the forward hunch of his shoulders and the explicit authority of his tread. Slipping in the front seat beside me and slamming the door, he radiated high tension off the hard, taut fibers of his face and his wild eyes that were red from sleeplessness, drink, chain-smoking, or maybe just unquenchable anger. He lit up immediately from a pack of cigarettes in his shirt pocket, after brusquely

121

giving me the name of a shacky disco not far from us back up OST. Taking a long drag on his cigarette and exhaling through his nose, he added, "And I need you to wait for me. I'm picking up a girl there."

It was a windowless, two-story structure, painted in a garish array of rainbow colors illuminated crudely by the few lights directed up at it from around the perimeter of the place, and stood alone in a large expanse of undeveloped land through which Old Spanish Trail made its course. To the north a few hundred yards were new apartment buildings sprinkled with the lights of those who had found recent abode there, and to the south, in the dark night, over the nearer darkness of a recently completed office complex, the black shadow of the Dome's great roof loomed in silhouette against the windy, cloud-scattered sky. It all made the narrow, woodframe premises of the club seem a strange, isolated island of hedonism in this blowy, grass-covered openness, a temporary mecca certainly destined for demolition once further modernization claimed this property.

I parked beyond the many cars already gathered in the lot, in the furthest corner from the door. "Now you wait, you hear. I don't know how long I will be, but just keep the timer going on your meter." He got out, throwing away the cigarette he had smoked en route, and lit up another as he walked aggressively from me, hunched and thin, his left hand in his pocket, and dragging hard on the cigarette he held in his right hand. He opened the door to a room bright with tangerine and lights, and rock music and people, then slammed it shut. The night abruptly re-enveloped me in its silence and its wind, and I waited.

At first I gazed at the neon advertising DANCE in one place, DISCO in another, and GIRLS in several places around the structure's exterior. I guess I didn't expect he would be long, so I kept my eyes in the direction of that door. The meter jumped every few moments, and eventually, as I tried to anticipate it, the sudden, loud metallic click even made me jump when it jarred the delicate balance I seemed to have become between the wide, sweeping forces of space and wind and time in their natural, patient course of the night, and what I increasingly worried might be something unnatural going on inside that club. He had come to pick up a girl, almost certainly not a customer who was meeting him there, but one of the dancers. Did he have it all arranged, or was he trying to do that now, and having difficulties? Or was he just enormously patient himself beneath that tight exterior of his, and expected me to be likewise?

The meter now read $10.00, all but $2.00 of it on the timer. The wind was blowing harder, coursing powerfully through the cab and across the fields of wild grass I imagined in the darkness waving like wheat under its thrust. The dark Dome was sentinel, and stage, and icon it seemed, for some vast drama its massive silence in the night held captive and purposeful for the clairvoyant who could understand it and read the wind. But my worry eclipsed such sensitive leanings and sensors in my soul. Dionysus and Apollo could have been wrestling in the black arena beneath the Dome, the ghosts of fifty thousand seats spell-bound at the contest, and the whole fate of the world really at stake in all this open silence of wind and sky and the dark side of the moon only one mile away, but increasingly I could only concern myself pettily with a customer running up a tab and calls over dispatch for trips I was not taking.

When the door opened and someone stumbled out, cutting through a gap to that bright, insulated interior that now revealed angry voices and some kind of untoward commotion, I got out and made my way across the parking lot to find out the story of my passenger. I opened the door on a loud, absurd scene. The Stones were belting out "Jumpin' Jack Flash" from multiple speakers, and slender girls in tangerine pasties and bikini pants, waving from their pulsing bodies gauzy swirls of tangerine scarves, were stacked in a helter-skelter arrangement of ledges up the far wall, but all of them, although trying to dance, gazing down transfixed at the confrontation toward the front of the room, where the tangerine paint of the interior towered up from us in an overwhelming monochrome, but still nothing to match the powerful, big-busted madam of the place in her heaped folds of tangerine chiffon waving her arms and streaming tangerine in a rage of color and words at the tall, thin, hunched figure of my passenger facing her off, while everyone else was in a hubbub and risen from their tables and backed against the walls and pointing and some of them shouting also. Beer bottles had spilled, and beer ran at my feet, then I saw a table over on its side and broken glass, and suddenly someone powerful had my arm. I looked abruptly sideways into the face of him who had to be the bouncer. "I'm a cabby. I brought him here. He asked me to wait."

"Get him out of here, before there's blood."

My passenger had seen me, and turned to shout, "I told you to wait. I'm not leaving yet. Not until she comes with me." The last remark was made with the clear intention everyone hear it, as his wild eyes ran around the room in utter defiance of the occupants. "Come on, honey," he now shouted at one of the girls, about halfway up the wall, who was immediately stopped, terrified in mid-motion of "Jumpin' Jack Flash, it's a gas" hoydenishly intoning the song's coda from the high speakers. Her eyes were those of a cornered animal, and her entire skinny slice of a body seemed impaled by his incredible gall to just haul her out of there.

"Look," I intervened, released by the bouncer so I could grab the arm of my passenger, "let's get out of here. There's going to be trouble."

"You can't buy my girls. They're dancers. They work for *me*!" the vast build of the madam yelled in a tower of tangerine-flying fury. "Get out! Get out! Who do you think you are? My girls are nice girls. I've told you again and again. Stop coming here. Now get out!" She was flapping her arms and chiffon like she was herding a flock of chickens, yet stood rooted to where she was, protecting her girls, but not venturing closer to my passenger.

Others were loudly repeating her words, "Get out!", over someone else saying, "Yes, nice girls, nice girls" in some kind of bizarre bass continuo to the rising cries of the crowd for his expulsion. But it was all just yet a medley of individual, unharmonized parts rather than a chorus, but slowly melding in that direction, toward eventual mass, dangerous hysteria and group-wielded, spontaneous violence.

"Look, let's get out of here," I pleaded again. "Let's go, you're not wanted. You need to rethink this."

"Honey, I'm taking you with me," he yelled decisively

toward her, over the head of the big, flapping tangerine bulk of the madam shouting, "Get out! Get out!", trying to herd us away with movements that made her arms look like great bat wings when she flapped them up and the chiffon flew out beneath.

I pulled on him, and he gave a little, forced to take a step back. I pulled harder, and he relinquished more ground. Then I had him out the door, when suddenly he tossed me aside. "I told you to wait," he said angrily.

"Yes, you did. But your life's in danger in there, and you owe me a considerable fare." I didn't know if that was a proper equation, but I was grasping for something angry and convincing to say. "Someone's going to get hurt, and you're going to be responsible. Now look, let's get back to the cab. Let me take you somewhere else. Otherwise pay me what you owe me and I'm gone."

He just burst back through the door and into the club again. Impulses and angry currents seized me now, and I charged in after him. The bouncer had grabbed hold of him this time, whatever patience in him exhausted, and the two were wrestling violently. The bouncer's fist flew, and my passenger landed bang against my chest. I latched onto him and hauled him again to the door. But suddenly all the previously bound-up fear and hesitation of those within, and madam at the center, came free at that one flying fist on my passenger's face, the whole lot of them surging forward in a mass, gloating fury for the kill. We almost fell back through the door, and I was hustling his now passive body through the parking lot as the door sprang open after us, disgorging the furies in pursuit. In the lead was the massive tangerine bat of the madam, arms and chiffon flapping wildly, as if trying to take flight for our two stumbling, humbled bodies weaving between the cars and making for the cab.

Somewhere in mid-parking lot the bouncer caught the fire-breathing dragon on our tail, and risked life and limb—as big as *he* was—against the fists of outrage she was beating and pummeling the air and him with, and the curses and fantastic volume of anger's drivel she heaved like wads of hissing spit in our direction. "I'll kill him, I'll kill him! I swear, I'll—" (the rest garbled and muffled in all that chiffon that seemed to have caught in her throat as the bouncer struggled against her).

Shoving my passenger in the cab I jumped behind the wheel and got out of there, squealing tires and careening wildly back onto OST and headed west. The last I saw, the entire crowd had emptied into the parking lot, even the skinnies in their pasties, and were watching us flee from behind the two figures still wrapped in gargantuan battle (and tangerine seeming to leap like flames over the sagging, bruised body of the bouncer slowly sinking under her fists to the asphalt). "I'll kill him, I swear!" roared its way to our ears, in one last triumph of volume and resolve overtaking cab 621 as we sped from the scene.

I was breathing heavily in jerks and spasms, ramming my foot on the accelerator. But my passenger just lay crumpled over on his side of the front seat, shriveled up like an insect hit with a torrent of poison spray.

"She loves me. I know she does," a voice finally managed meekly from that mess of a man beside me. "We agreed it would be tonight. I would take her tonight."

"Or is that just what you told her you would do?" I said in exasperated reply.

"She loves me. I know she does."

We were approaching the station where I had picked him up. "Well, what now?" I said. "Where do I take you? Do you live here, or are you staying somewhere? Let me take you home, or to your hotel, or wherever."

"I'm in a motel."

"Well, where is it? I'll take you there."

"I can't. My wife's there."

With that I just pulled into the station. I didn't know what else to do, and stopped off to the side.

"Take me back," he said, his voice resurrecting that peremptory tone of before. "Take me back. I'm not leaving without her."

"Oh no you don't. I'm taking you no further. You go back there and you'll get killed. Or someone. Just admit the situation for Godssakes."

"She loves me. I know she does," he said, burying his head in his hands and suddenly starting to cry.

When finally I got him out of the cab, after he passively let me count out from his wallet, stashed thick with greenbacks, the amount owed me, he stumbled a moment, lit up a cigarette, and stood dazed. "Hey you!" an attendant shouted suddenly, appearing at the door of his office, "can't you see there's No Smoking signs all over the place. This is a gas station."

He stared at the man, seemed to wobble a bit, like he was drunk, then threw the cigarette down and stomped on it. I watched from inside the cab as he turned and walked back in the direction we'd come, disappearing in the darkness. I swung 621 around, thinking to catch him and stop him someway, but at that moment he reappeared, back into the glary light of the station, walking more deliberately now, pondering.

When I left he was walking aggressively back and forth, shoulders hunched forward, and staring down directly in front of him. He reached once for the pack of cigarettes in his shirt pocket, but stopped, apparently remembering, and kept pacing.

What he was thinking seemed no more calculable than the immense shadow of the Astrodome looming to my left as I drove away. Mute, its void somehow an unremitting contest deciding fateful things in all its vast, black capacity before empty seats.

Aphrodite

The place hardly looked honky-tonk. It was just a little grey box. But XXXX on Westheimer packed a show that had men agog and near crazed when they left the place. Late one afternoon I picked up a fellow there who was headed back to Washington, D.C., and the sweat of his excitement was like a glaze off his balding head and flabby countenance, and positively jumping through his dark blue, pinstripe suit in black blotches of seepage spreading everywhere. "Oh man, do those girls know how to pump it out!" he exulted from the middle of the back seat, jabbing piston-like his fisted right hand rapidly forward and back. "That beats anything I've seen in D.C."

I was repelled enough I didn't say anything, all the way to his hotel downtown to retrieve his bags, then on to the airport. But I had Houston commuters to deal with anyway, and he grew officious and fussy over papers he pulled from his briefcase as I fought our way north up I45. By the time I got him to his terminal at Intercontinental he was the model lawyer absorbed in his brief to be delivered the next day, the pink of his face had even matured to a certain sallow color, and I could imagine him returning to family and home in a pleasant Washington suburb. XXXX had become subcortical and reserved for another visit I suppose.

But it was the same with all the men I took from that bunker-like structure, all of them florid and flashing with sweat on leaving the place, reeking of beer usually, and from the back seat bouncing hosannas of praise for the feats of female pyrotechnics they had witnessed. Forced to endure their manic ravings I learned the girls were black, and young, and that they stripped to full nudity on that little stage, writhing and posturing in graphic simulations of the sex act that drove the men wild and panting right up and over the proscenium apparently, in hot male bother and beery boisterousness for more, more.

But I didn't want to know. And usually there seemed a state of shock my passengers underwent as the world outside soaked in, embarrassment, guilt, amazement, whatever, but they de-evolved from all that high musk into a fidgety presence behind me, finally a subdued and passive one. They'd go silent after a time.

They were usually visitors, most of whom, unlike the lawyer, I took back to cheap motels along seedy streets. But I had the impression that like him they were married too, escaping too, but in their case to be returned to the fold of some quiet hearth in a small Texas town, the woman waiting there for them, maybe in nightgown and curlers when meeting them at the door, and that they would pass into the house both screaming deep inside and sighing relief. The door would then close for a while on their flabby, fidgety lives.

But impressions are impressions—a cab driver amasses

many, maybe many more than he has business to believe true—and still I had never seen the inside of XXXX or managed any kind of truth about those who worked there.

Then one night I was called to the place at 2:00 AM. Closing time. There was an understanding about the joint that we didn't go to the door. As soon as a cab appeared the door would open ajar, perhaps the bouncer making sure, then out would hurry our passenger. Besides, the place was right around the corner from the Westheimer One cab stand, and when they called they could count on a cab arriving immediately and have our fare waiting for us. The door of XXXX was sacred, or it was profane; either way not a single driver I knew had even been out of his cab to approach it.

So I waited. But the door remained closed. Getting impatient I finally got out and went up to find my passenger. I knocked first, but no response. So in I went. I found myself in the tiniest room, with a little square window and counter rather low in the wall in front of me, opening into a second tiny room also partitioned off from the club inside. A tallish white girl with frizzed, frantic-looking hair was bending down to peer at me from the other side of the window. I had to bend down myself to see her clearly. "Cab," I said. "Someone called."

"Look," she said, "you've got to get her home without them knowing where she lives. You've got to lose them. Understand?"

"Lose who? What do you mean?"

"They're a bunch of country drunks, and she did some-thing she shouldn't have, though they deserved it. But they told her they're going to get her. They kept going 'Bang, bang' before we could get them out of here. They're out back right now, waiting in their truck."

"Well, call the police."

"No, we don't want the police, see? Bring your cab up close, and lose them. They're drunk, but they're no joke."

"But where's the bouncer? Can't he help?"

"The creep, he left. Said he'd done his work for the night."

"Oh terrific," I muttered, trying to think. "All right, give me sixty seconds, then send her out. I'll have the cab door open, and we'll make tracks."

Quickly I positioned the cab snug to the entrance, and opened the passenger door opposite me in direct line with the door of the club, hardly finding time to realize how nervous I was. And out she came, an attractive young black under a mass of snaky hair, wearing a pert red cocktail dress that whispered of silk as she slid quickly in the front seat and slammed the door. And I was gone, finding how nervous I was the way I squealed rubber, right around in a tight U-turn and out into Westheimer, headed east.

She said nothing, just stared straight ahead, rigidly clasping a little purse in her lap. Then suddenly into my rearview mirror jumped the headlights of a large pickup truck. I saw only shadows, but a crowd of them was standing in the bed, holding cowboy hats to their heads and shouting after us a volley of four-letter words. "Cunt" was the one I heard most often and loud. They were gunning it for my rear and I gunned it to make the Montrose light.

It changed red as I got there, and I hurled my cab around in a skidding, screaming U, dead center in the intersection. A chorus of horns from the cars stopped on Montrose greeted my efforts, but I just rammed the accelerator again, hoping a police car was among them. The pickup threw itself into a repeat of my maneuver, but further into the intersection, and nearly crashed against the far curb, keeping the horn section fortissimo in my wake. Checking my mirror I saw the bullish headlights of the truck wobbling up to speed again, and the cowboy types swaying crazily, as they came on in fresh pursuit.

I swung a sharp left near the Tower Theater, then another sharp left, down the length of a parking lot fronting a supermarket and bank. The truck raced past us the other way, and succeeded in duplicating my tracks with a lot of roaring and huffing as I came out of the parking lot blaring my own horn and blasting across the Montrose intersection this time, right through the red light and amazed melee of cars.

I will admit it, I was getting into rhythm here, in a major key at the finesse of our escape, and flew up the eastern length of Westheimer sure they would never catch us, riding a pulse of strings all più presto and resplendent in my head at the power I felt, even pumping the horn staccato and almost slaphappy to warn cross traffic at the one light we encountered, though fortunately it was green. But suddenly there they were again in my mirror, heaving after us and gaining. I hadn't shaken them. Only then did I realize how serious they were, drunk or not. The gang rape, even murder, of the woman beside me had hardly seemed possible before. But those headlights looked deadly now, the symphony and rush of my earlier surge of adrenaline now churning to a minor key—at last shredding under the pounding of "Bang, bang" reaching our ears in a sinister two-note ostinato from some of them back there, and "We'll finish you, babe," and "We're comin', comin', all over you, nigger cunt," from the others in a jeering refrain getting closer, closer.

"You're just meat, and each of us's goin' to have you! You're done!" the driver leaned out his window and shouted.

Then a new sound emerging through it all, filling the cab with an eerie gossamer texture. I glanced at the woman beside me. Her mouth was open, and from her throat a high quavering of terror, light as breath, lifted between her parted teeth. Like the tremulous, floating wail of the sleeper locked in the throes of nightmare, unable to escape, trapped and at the mercy of the mind's worst fears coming on with heartless unstoppability. Unless I could dispel it.

But how? They looked about to ram our rear, and I pushed away with a burst of speed. But ahead was Houston's Mid-Town, stoplights and cross traffic I couldn't possibly barrel through, even at this hour, without the likelihood of broadsiding someone at some point. Only one reprieve: the bend in Westheimer on the Mid-Town border, where it veered to the right and widened to become Elgin at the Bagby Street intersection. Though one-way the wrong way, Bagby was wide. Just enough space, if I hurled a left from the far right lane I was in, and if no one was coming. I had only an instant to look, but no one coming down Bagby, no one anywhere, and through a red light over I went, braking madly just to make the turn, in a torture of tires and spinning and levitation that almost seemed a kind of sleep, heeling us up into the air as the cab's left tires lifted just so much from the road in a wide floating arc, circumscribed by her wail reaching now to horror, and I only audience anymore to the titanic screech and whine and dream-craziness of this symphony and motion now into finale and coda. The pickup screaming too, in a sideways skid behind us.

But they didn't make it. Turning too late in the intersection the driver hit the far curb this time, the thudding crash of percussion signaling the abrupt end of the coda. The smoke of brakes and rubber filled the air with stench, and I swung us about in the gagging cloud, at least headed the right way on Bagby now. The last I saw of that truck its headlights were positioned one above the other, and quite stopped. Bodies and hats sprawled everywhere beyond the upended bed, across a small lot, and only the spinning front tire in the air to bring the performance to a pianissimo, and pleasing, finish. Applause broke out everywhere in my head—Berlioz couldn't have done it better. I couldn't help it, I cried "Bravo" at the top of my lungs at the sudden release and triumph I felt, repeating it several times in the direction of those bodies. Then I ducked out of there, not wanting the police when they came, crossing the bend in Westheimer and disappearing up a side street from Bagby. Some distance away, along a quiet block, I rolled to a halt.

I looked at her. Her eyes remained transfixed on the windshield, and she clutched her purse tightly, but her bosom swelled and let go in deep audible breaths as she struggled for calm, down the register of all the suspense and fright finally over, the rhythm and life of her breathing overwhelmingly sensuous to my awakened, reeling senses, still wild with victory on her behalf. Studying her like that, this unknown woman so vulnerable moments ago, I saw that she was beautiful. Her long black hair fell in a kinky, wild tumbling over her shoulders and the spaghetti straps of her red dress, framing a mulatto bronze face that was striking. I realized it was a strong face, it was proud. "Thank you," she said at last, in a quiet, shaky voice. And she repeated it several times, her tone slowly gaining resonance as she collected herself. "I thought maybe. . . maybe I was going to die. But you must be a stuntman on the side." And she giggled girlishly, glancing at me out of her long lashes and shaking her head. "Yes, you must be." It was odd, but beguiling, that she could laugh now. After all that. Almost erotic, in the deep night and quiet, the peace suddenly, that was ours.

She gave me her address, and brief directions to get there, an apartment complex off Alabama in the Third Ward, and I noted how her voice was rounded by an accent I couldn't recognize, slightly nasal, but melodious. The meter flag over, we were finally a legitimate cab trip, and I headed south for Alabama through the dark, sleeping neighborhood encompassing us. But in the ensuing silence I kept looking at her. The bond I felt for this woman after our ordeal was almost too much. Finally I saw her looking at me. "What is your name?" I asked, something I never did with passengers.

"It is not a common name," she replied. "I have a Greek name. I am called Aphrodite. But I come from Brazil."

"Aphrodite? I know a goddess by that name." And at that I blushed, but hoped it was not evident in the dark.

"Well, it's only because like her I first came from the sea. My birthplace was the sea."

"Really? Yours must be an unusual story: from the sea, from Brazil, and up here of all places, in this city of too many Anglos and cowboys. Though at least we have the sea too, which is the better part of what this city's about."

"Well," she replied, "my story is unusual, and then maybe not. Actually, I was born on a ferry, from Recife to Rio. My mother was trying to get to her sister's before delivery, but I came before she could get there. She was not married, and was alone on the trip. And poor. I was born on the deck. My aunt was told other women traveling deck class assisted her. But a storm came. The ferry had too many people, or was too old. I don't know, but it sank in the waves. I was plucked from my mother as she went down. No one could save her I guess, but I ended up in a lifeboat. When I was brought at last to my aunt in Rio, she named me. It was her idea that Aphrodite was a kind of godmother to me. I have no idea who my father was, nor did my aunt. I grew up in one of the *favelas*, the shantytowns, in the south of the city. My aunt was poor, but she raised me. She worked hard for me, made sure I had schooling, and made me study English. As beautiful as *Portugués* is, she said I had to know English. She arranged for a Baptist missionary, a young man from here in Texas who lived among us and had a small church, to teach me. Because I had to be cosmopolitan, my aunt said, to escape the *favelas* someday, maybe come to the States even. Of course in time the young missionary took more of an interest in me than tutoring English, or imparting his faith, but I never told my aunt. Life was hard enough for her. Her husband had died, and her two children. I was all she had, even if I had to do some growing up of my own without her knowledge. Then when I was older she arranged for me to work in a wealthy home across the city. And it was while I was away working for those people, only two years ago, that her shanty went up in flames, a big fire that burned the whole hillside. She and many others were killed. I lost her. I had no one anymore."

I marveled at her quiet, firm voice, that seemed so eloquent to me—and after what she had just been through, and being an orphan, so far from her land. It chastened me, looking at her, hearing her, and I winced at what I realized had been a kind of condescension in my feeling of triumph for her sake. That I had saved her. I had been lucky was all, and the credit somehow seemed hers, not mine. "How did you end up here, and working back at that place? It's certainly a long way from home for you."

"I came here seven weeks ago, almost exactly, with a businessman from São Paulo. I was his mistress. He had seen me walking the beach of Ipanema one day. I was dressed plainly of course, but I had looks. It had become a consolation for me to walk by the sea when I had time off from the family I worked for. Well, he approached me, made his advances. I thought, why not? I wasn't going anywhere in life. My aunt was gone, and maybe I could use my looks. So I just disappeared from that family. After a few days in a fancy Rio hotel, he took me back to São Paulo and set me up in an apartment. He was married, but he kept it all very discreet. Then he brought me with him to Houston on a business trip. He was into land development in Brazil's interior, and was swinging some deal here. We stayed at a hotel over in the Galleria. He knew I no longer liked him very much, and he was trying to impress me with this trip. He was in meetings all day, for a whole week; and I met this boy. I would watch everyone skating on the rink, in the center of the mall. I had never seen skating before, and this boy was beautiful to watch on his skates. He was shy, not a man yet, his voice just breaking. But he was home for spring break from some prep school in Connecticut, his family quite wealthy. I brought him up to my room. He was a virgin, but I taught him. We met up there every morning after that, before the room was made up, so Rui would come back from his meetings and find the room cleaned and not suspect anything. But the last day I wouldn't let my young lover go, and Rui returned early to discover us.

"You can guess what happened. The boy cleared out of there before he was beat up. But Rui beat me savagely, then checked out and left me, with only a little money in my purse. He even took my return ticket with him. I never saw the boy again. His name was James. He's back to his school. I called his home number he had given me; for several days I tried to reach him, but his family suspected something was going on they didn't like, and shielded him from me until he left. I could never talk to him. Once again I had no one. I was out in the street. Well, I'm a little streetwise growing up where I did, and I'll fend for myself. I needed money fast, and found work at that place where you picked me up.

"I have a passport and a suitcase of fancy clothes. But now I have something else too. It means everything to me. I refused to believe it until this week. But now I know for sure. And this week I put on a show like I never had before in that place, knowing what I had that was mine. That I was no longer alone. And I laughed, I worked it into my act, I laughed, even stripped in front of all those men. I didn't care. And I danced. Like they do at Carnaval. The *maxixe*, the samba, even some bossa nova. And I sang too, the *canções* that go way back in our folklore. The manager complained that I didn't imitate sex enough in my movements. He said I danced too much. He wanted me to stop singing. But I didn't care. Then one of those men in that truck, with his cowboy hat on and tipsy because he was drunk, came up to the stage and squirted beer all over me as I was finishing my last set tonight. And you know what I did? I kicked him in the face. Hard. Maybe broke his nose. A naked woman kicked him in the face in front of all his friends."

"But you can't go back to work there now. It's not safe. They may come back, or at least one of them not too busted up by that crash."

"No. I'm not going back. I have just enough money now. I've saved, just enough to make it to Recife, where my mother came from. I've never been there. But I'm going. I already have a ticket for Rio in two days. I'm going. I'm carrying that boy's child, you see."

"Oh. But. . . are you. . . are you sure it's his?" Then I felt embarrassed.

But she just laughed lightheartedly. "I understand why you ask that. But it's not Rui's. He was too clean. He didn't want me pregnant. But with that boy I wanted the chance. And it happened. I'm going to have this baby. James will never know. But he was only fourteen, and has a different life in front of him. It's for the best. And I'll go down to the sea, to the beach at Boa Viagem—I've always wanted to see Boa

Viagem—and bathe with my child in the surf. Recife will be our home. It will be a way of finding my mother again; and my aunt would understand. I find myself filled now with what we call in my language *saudade*. It's a feeling of wanting to return, of what you call nostalgia, longing. But for us it's a good feeling, one we can act on. I know I can make it happen. And I'll get work of some kind. Good work. My English will help. Maybe I can be a translator. But good work. Enough of men for now," she added emphatically. "I just want my baby. I have someone now."

A moment later I pulled up beside her apartment complex, and watched her walk away, this orphan of the sea, her figure confident and rather tall beneath the light of a single lamppost shining down on the vast locks of her hair and the shimmering silk of her cocktail dress. In the night's silence the click of her high heels sounded precise and crisp on the pavement. She had said "Thank you" one more time to me as she pressed an extra five dollars in my hand. "I will remember you. You too are also father to this child, in a way, because without you it might never have been born. I owe you two lives." And she had kissed me. Only then did I smell the faintness of the beer that had been squirted over her.

Now I could only watch as she climbed a set of iron stairs, her heels loud on the rungs, to the second floor. She pulled a key from her purse, opened the door on a dark room, and turned to wave, before disappearing inside. A light came on through the closed curtain.

It issued quietly from my lips as I sat there a little longer: "Bravo, bravo." Though I hoped somehow it would reach her.

Tiara

River Oaks gave one an eerie feeling sometimes. For me, driving elsewhere in the city most of the night, to enter its intersecting streets of abundance was to be engulfed in a kind of darkness, a feeling most people who lived there would surely have thought irrational, or just resentful. But the expensive homes were like fortresses at night, set back from the wide streets like big blocks. The nosegays of light from lamps flanking the strong doors, or the muted, hued light from behind closed curtains, even the streetlamps themselves, shed at best an enfeebled glow against the high expansive darkness of facade after facade, and against the shrubbery and trees of precise landscaping that were only a heavy and attendant gloom of their own. The streets didn't live here at night, and what did was locked within the closure of the huge homes, where the wealthy could now turn their back to the city that made their fortune.

Was it the little story "Araby" by James Joyce I had been reading this afternoon that seduced me into this place? (I kept myself reading the two hours or so before leaving for the cab lot, to shore up my sanity that with a college degree I continued doing this for a living, seeking romance where nothing else sufficed but the wheel of my yellow cab.) I recalled the story's description of North Richmond Street, its houses that "conscious of decent lives within them, gazed at one another with brown, imperturbable faces." But children played on that street into the night, their shouts and games claimed its blind, dead-ended length. But not a soul to be seen here, and these streets weren't even blind, but led everywhere into the city, and the world beyond, an odd inversion that fascinated and disturbed me this evening. River Oaks, far from the poverty of Joyce's little street, seemed a Janus of prosperity in its Roman proportions, but with the face gone that looked out, replaced by the staunch front doors locked and shut, and the other face only looking in, where air-conditioned, dry, free of humidity and enclosed, rich River Oaks turned all its light in on itself. While on the outside the lawns, the streets, and even the wet stars floating so high above in the moist Gulf sky, were a dark, abandoned stage. The sense of absence in it gripped me tonight.

Whether it was the Dublin in my veins, and the failed, romantic longing of the story's young hero, that at least was longing, was hope, I couldn't say, but coming south across the Buffalo Bayou from out Washington Avenue, where I had dropped off a passenger—a young Hispanic male who had worked late at the Southern Pacific rail yard north of downtown—some impulse, maybe only of vanity, had urged me to enter these streets, rather than make straight for my accustomed haunt this time of night up Westheimer in the Montrose district. Maybe I was hoping for someone going to the airport, someone to have to exit from their front door and reach me parked on the street, though nothing was coming from dispatch for this area. They certainly would never use a cab for anything else, except to send a maid home. But the maids were all home now, returned to the poverty of their lives out East End, or in the Third Ward.

Embarrassed at my folly for wandering around here, losing time on a night when I desperately needed to make some cash—tips, I needed tips—I at last made for Westheimer in search of a fare. I was just short of the brightly lit boulevard that bordered River Oaks on the south, still in the darkness of the last block of all this affluence, when I saw two figures on the sidewalk ahead to my right.

It was like a shadow play, two bodies in some kind of entanglement silhouetted against the light of Westheimer, but vicious, as I saw the long arm of one of them unleash a jab and sock the other flat to the sidewalk. I drove up and stopped at the curb. A young woman in an evening gown of white was sprawled and holding her white gloved arms up before a tall gentleman in black tuxedo who delivered a brutal kick right to her stomach. I heard her yelped cry of pain and jumped from my cab, leaving the door wide open as I rushed at the man.

"Stop, for Godssakes," I yelled. But he had pulled her from the sidewalk and now slapped her hard across the face— like a whip crack it sprung the muggy air. She slumped, but he reached back a second time to deliver an even harsher blow. I stretched my arm out straight as he swung at her, and the thudding crunch of his arm on mine, like the jarring shock of two swords, sent him reeling back and her falling from his grasp to the sidewalk. I grabbed my stinging arm.

"What the hell are you doing?" I shouted at him. He turned to look at me, holding his own arm where it had cracked against mine, and in the penumbra of my headlights I saw he was almost a youngster. Just twenty, if that. He noted my cab behind me, with its For Hire sign illuminated on the roof. "Take her. Get her out of here," he said in a slow, malevolent voice over the quick panting of his chest. "Before I kill her. You hear me, get her out of here."

We were hunched like apes toward one another over the body of the woman. He was blond, handsome, but his lower jaw jutting out at me, revealing teeth and slobber of his anger that jumped at me in drops from his rapid, ugly breathing, gave him a vampirish look that was horrible and odd for one so young and elegantly attired, All American. I smelled the raw stink of alcohol on his breath.

"Yes, I'll get her out of here. But you get yourself out of here." My anger surged as I spoke, my hands becoming fists, even as he seemed to cool off. He straightened himself up, making himself quite tall, as he looked in disgust down at the woman. She lay there limp, just a bundle of an exquisite dress with a leg sticking out up to the thigh. A face was buried somewhere, crying in heavy, jerking sobs. The young man then lifted his leg coldly and slowly for a last kick at all that satin and lace, the coup de grâce. I threw myself at him like a blocker, into his chest, and sent him flying back at the instant his foot cracked into my shin. He ended up on all fours, but pulled himself up and turned to send an arc of spit onto the bundle at my feet. Then he walked away, in a slightly uneven gait crossing the street, back into the dark of River Oaks. In a moment I heard tires squeal, as a decade-old

Chevy ripped around in a U-turn and charged by us with a blast of the horn. Then he swung to the right onto Westheimer, squealing tires again in a wide swerving across lanes, shimmying to straighten up, before gone.

I picked her up, trying to help her stand and adjust the confusion of her dress. The face that emerged was stunningly young and beautiful—even marred with tears and a swollen, purplish cheek, and a split lower lip where blood coursed down her chin, as it also did from the corner of her mouth. I pulled my handkerchief from my back pocket and offered it to her. She accepted it with a nod of her head and pressed it to her mouth to stop the bleeding, which had already spotted her dress. Suddenly a fresh jolt of anguish and sobs rocked her frame, and she clenched her teeth hard to stop it. I just stood there transfixed. She was like a queen out of some fairy-tale ball: her blond, coiffured hair carried a little diamond tiara askew but still pinned, and over everything her perfume was a rush on my senses. Her décolletage revealed thin but shapely shoulders that quivered from the spastic heaving of her breast in a manner poignant but not pathetic. She was organizing herself quickly in fact, taking deep breaths to control and stop her crying. She looked back at my cab with its For Hire sign. "I don't have any money to pay you, but can you take me home?" she said in a soft, almost whispered voice.

"Certainly. No, please, keep the handkerchief," as she seemed uncertain whether she should return it, stained in blood as it was. "But you need a doctor. Let me take you to a doctor first."

"No, please. I'll be all right. Just take me home."

"Well, if you wish, of course I will. But look, we should call the police. I have a radio and—"

"No, no!" she gasped in alarm, putting those gloved arms up as if I were striking her. "No." Then more calmly: "He's my husband."

My heart sank. But she just turned to locate her small purse on the sidewalk behind her. Then, in a kind of defiance of the pain evident in her every move, wobbling in her silver-tinted high heels and looking like she might fall, she walked to the cab, its engine still running, and, leaning against the back door a moment, opened it with effort and swung herself unsteadily onto the seat. I hadn't even moved from my spot when she closed the door. My shin smarted, and my arm throbbed. Maybe it was the impotence of the moment, or the fact she put such a determined face on it now awaiting me behind that door, but suddenly practical thoughts overwhelmed me. Would I pay her way? No, I concluded, not if she lived at any distance. I had made nothing in tips tonight, my passengers so far too poor, and after buying groceries today had started my shift with little cash of my own. And everything earned off the meter had to be handed over once I returned to the lot. Unless she lived very close I would have to take her with the meter off and that For Hire sign on the roof bright as a beacon. Which was illegal, we'd been told and indoctrinated aggressively at orientation, the police would stop us with a passenger aboard and that sign on, and we'd be fired.

Unsteady myself from the bruise to my shin, I went around locking the other doors and making sure the windows were up, explaining to her it was to prevent someone trying to board the cab at a stoplight with its For Hire sign on. I slipped in the cab and locked my own door. Then learning her address was over toward Mid-Town, on Richmond, through the Montrose district that was always heavily patrolled this time of night, I asked her to lie down in the back so she would not be noticeable. She complied obediently, and started crying the moment she did.

You've become city-wise and cold, I told myself. I pulled away from the curb and made a left on Westheimer, headed east, rolling my own window up and turning the air-con on low as I listened to her crying from deep in the back seat where I had forced her to hide. You've lost your honor. How can you even take her to such a home anyway? "How can I take you home?" I said. "He'll come back."

"Not for a couple of days," she replied feebly through her tears. "Just take me home, please. He has a friend he goes to, a young man from work who puts him up when he gets like this."

"You mean this has happened before?"

There was a silence, her sobs receding as if she was staring some revelation in the face. "Maybe I'll go home. This. . . this the last time. Catch a bus, and just go."

"Do you have any family here you can call?"

"No, not here. Only Danny's uncle he's working for. He's been good to me, but he's a big man, short of temper, and I'm afraid what he'd do to Danny if he knew this." A moment passed. "But I have my mother. In Eden—Eden, Texas. A small town out west, near San Angelo. That's where I'm from. And my husband."

Her voice seemed a soft talking from some great depth,

of sorrow, of wisdom. I could hear the rustling of her dress back there as she wrestled with realities. "Back to Eden. I was Homecoming Queen. But he'd graduated a year earlier, and waited around till I graduated so we could get married. We were celebrating our first wedding anniversary tonight, having dinner at a fancy place out on the west side as a gift from Danny's uncle. And that's why this silly crown of fake diamonds. Mine for being Homecoming Queen. He wanted me like that tonight. He'd been the quarterback his senior year."

"Sounds like a classic teen-age wedding." You've become city-wise and cold, I told myself again. Watch your sarcasm.

"Yes, everyone warned us against it. No one more than my mother." The tears had stopped. Her voice was firmer now, in grips with the truth it seemed. "He can't handle this city. He should have gone to college. Instead he came here to work for his uncle, in landscaping, to support me. Just a laborer, that's what he's been. He's tried, I know, and he's kept saying he'd be more, just give him time. Be his uncle's manager, or have his own business even. Make it big for his 'perfect wife.' That's what he likes to call me, his 'perfect wife.'" She was struggling to speak, her voice becoming increasingly blurred from the injuries to her mouth, her words forcing themselves out from deeper in her throat. "That's why we were in River Oaks. After our dinner he wanted to walk around and look at all the impressive homes. Trying to impress me with what he could do some day. It's always been a question of what he could do, not me. He won't let me work—all year I've wanted to, but he's said no. That's why the argument. While we were walking I asked him still again to let me go to work, and I. . . I got upset this time when he said no. I told him I felt caged, useless, and he. . . he blew up. It was like I insulted him. I didn't mean to hurt his feelings. But he, he'd had too much to drink. That's the worst he's ever been. I keep thinking, if we'd both just gone to college."

"But why didn't you?"

"Danny couldn't get a football scholarship—he wasn't a great quarterback, and Eden's a small school anyway—and he just wouldn't go without that scholarship. Then he begged me not to go. Marry him, and we'd make it on our own. He didn't want the campus—Angelo State, that's where I wanted to go, and we could just afford it—he didn't want any campus, not without football. And he had this stubborn idea he deserved a scholarship if he played." She stopped a moment. It had to be physically painful for her to speak so much. "He's good with his hands, that's what he knows," she continued. "Kind of old-fashioned, I guess. But. . . but there's a sweetness you know. Or was. . ." She had raised her head somewhat to speak, but with her last words I heard her head fall to the seat, a whispering of her twisted dress as her body coiled around back there, and with a snatch in her throat she let out a cry of anguish. "This city, it's just crushed him. Houston's crushed him. Too big, everyone anonymous. We've been living out of yearbook memories for months now, he always pointing to my graduation picture and talking of his 'perfect wife.' Drinking, drinking more and more, and becoming. . ." —she took a deep breath—"becoming what you saw just now."

We made upper Westheimer, with its raucous night life,

153

the glare of neon flowing by, and people wandering the streets looking for something to do, a new bar or strip joint, a new thrill. All just flowing by. Somehow she gave this trip a complete insularity. It struck me only now that I could have taken back streets, and not forced her to lie down and hide. Yet I'd taken a central thoroughfare. It brought to mind the boy in "Araby" again, the image of him carrying the chalice that was the girl he loved safely "through a throng of foes" as he believed, negotiating the ugly, crowded night streets of Dublin in triumph for her sake. As if I were doing the same— the story with its cruel failure of adolescent love entwining like a serpent even my sense of judgment tonight—as if I too were triumphant taking this girl safely down the bustling, ugly corridor of Westheimer against the odds, in but a vain parade of chauvinism made worse by forcing her to hide behind me in an abject manner that was all contradiction. What was I doing? Suddenly I was afraid for her again, once I dropped her off. I saw him kicking her in the stomach again, slapping her senseless. Would he have killed her as he claimed? All American, and amok with hate.

"Maybe you shouldn't go home. Let's figure something else out. He might come back."

"Just take me home please." Maybe it was the note of command, even in that voice now marred and swollen from her injuries, but a kind of awe overcame me when she said this.

"You're pretty remarkable, you know that?"

"No, nothing remarkable, please. Please. Nothing. . ." Her voice trailed off.

"But why, why does he do this to you?" I wailed. "Why

does he hurt you?"

"Because, don't you see, none of it's come true," she said, pushing her head up to give strength to her voice, that seemed to float up balloon-like, without contours, from her forcing out the words that her mouth could barely shape anymore. "A storybook life. That's what my mother said, we were trying to be a storybook life, and she cautioned me against it, especially if we left home. But Danny had to be big enough for a place like this. When he gave up on football without a scholarship, he had to be big in some other way. His uncle was shorthanded here, with a lot of business, some of it in River Oaks. And he won't hire Hispanics or blacks. So he offered Danny a job. It seemed to Danny a chance better than anything else, and reason to get married, since he could support me. His father runs a small grocery in Eden, and could hardly pay him enough, and Danny didn't want to be a farm hand. He said he wanted the city, it was the big chance for both of us. Don't you see, it's because of me, trying to live up to the dream he promised me. His 'perfect wife,' at least when he could believe it of me. But I'm not perfect, just a woman in love with him is all. His Homecoming Queen, but he doesn't believe anymore. I'm not perfect. . . just wanting to work, be normal and learn things. Even in a grocery store if I could." Her head fell back down to the seat, and a long weary sigh gagged momentarily on a sob.

That moment I came to the Montrose light and stopped, waiting to make a right turn behind another car with a crowd milling at the corner. Someone tried to open the door opposite me, then the back door. I turned to see two muscular males in tight jeans, both of whom began banging on the cab to let them in. She gave a cry of alarm, and pushed herself up. "No, stay down," I commanded. "Motherfucker, let us in," one of them yelled. "Fuckin' cabbies in this town," the other added, bringing the flat of his hand down hard on the trunk and starting to rock the back of the car. The first was around trying to open my door. When he found it locked, he banged away at my window.

"Motherfucker! Motherfucker!"

With tiny frightened breaths she remained gripped to the back seat in this island of space we could claim, and I slammed the flat of my hand against the inside of my window. "Get away from my cab. I'm taking no fares." The one behind was still rocking the cab violently with all his strength, and his companion replied with a thwack on my window that sounded like it broke the glass. Then the light turned green, the car ahead of me moved, and I knocked the two of them off with a jam on my accelerator and a squealing turn away from there.

"It's all right. It's all right now," I assured her. Headed south on Montrose, I slowed down after a block. It wasn't far now to her place, and I wanted to delay the trip as long as possible. "I'm sorry for that back there. I should have gone another way. Look, why don't you sit up. This is foolish, that I made you lie down. Foolish I didn't take a different route. Please, sit up."

She popped right up, the silhouette of her head, complete with tiara, filling my rearview mirror. She looked around at the passing city, as if she were someone just waking up, then blew her nose. "I guess I've ruined your handkerchief. I'm sorry."

"That's quite all right. That's what they're for."

It was remarkable, but she seemed strong all of a sudden, upright like that, simply upright, now that I no longer denied her any dignity by forcing her down. In my mirror I saw her gazing calmly out one side and then the other at the sights of this city that had only come to mean pain. We were beyond the honky-tonk, and the cafes and crowds here, though bohemian, reflected the University of St. Thomas nearby and the museum district further on. A world of coffee bars, discussion and art. A greater elegance that didn't deny her, but gave our passage now a kind of freedom. Opportunity in life was still there for her, I thought, and I swelled suddenly with pride at the sight of her silhouette in my mirror. In the simplicity of what she was, a girl—dressed up as a Homecoming Queen and treated as a toy doll an abusive husband could break or smash as he wished—she seemed a woman back there, and it was my turn to cry as tears sprouted in my eyes, a lump formed in my throat, at the beauty and innocence of her petite figure sitting up, a queen surely. Perfect. That word now flashed through my brain brighter than any For Hire sign riding my roof.

But utterly alone. Vulnerable. He was coming back. And our journey over in moments.

"Do you have a life to go back to?" I asked. "In Eden I mean."

"My mother. I lost my father when I was young, to cancer. But I have my mother. She came to visit us Christmas, and it was nice then. She has just enough from my father's pension, and tends her flowers there. We've missed each other. It's been hard. We write all the time." The swelling of her mouth had reached a point that her voice was forced into a plaintive, nasal quality, high-pitched over the mumble of her actual words, like a young child might speak if it had the vocabulary.

"Is there work you can do in Eden?"

"I've told her with her knowledge of flowers she could open a small florist shop. I could help her." I swung into the left turn lane at the Richmond intersection.

"It really would be good to see Eden and Mom again."

"Well damn him, he can stay behind and look after himself from now on. He deserves that."

"No, no. Don't say that." A choke in her throat and I regretted I spoke. "You don't understand. He'll never forgive himself for what he did. He'll come back all broken up. He'll never make it alone. It'll kill him if I leave."

"But he nearly killed *you!*"

"Please, just take me home. Get me home."

Her head was bobbing, her mouth gaping, and she fought the battle—grief sweeping her. Grief as much for him as for herself. She was not divorced from him at all. In our cab our tiny passage of freedom was ultimately chained as much to the guilt and burden of responsibility she felt for what he'd become, as to the man himself, now on a drunken rampage somewhere in the western part of the city. The light changed, and when clear I swung a left onto Richmond. Her apartment complex only two blocks away.

Now my feelings were a battle. What to do to break the chain? He would someday go too far. He had said it, after all: he would kill her.

The ride was over. I stopped. My thoughts were in a race,

spinning wheels trying to grab a surface somewhere. Anything to break the chain, save her. Could I take her to my own place, and find somewhere else for me to stay? She would never stay if I were there. Could I call some friends to give her a place? Because she can't stay here. She can't. She can't stay with him.

But she had already unlocked and opened her door, gotten out. I opened mine and turned to her. "Thank you," she said, standing before me, handkerchief in one hand, and little gold purse in the other. "You were kind, very kind." Her words of gratitude, so low and misshapen from her throat, wrenched me in my seat as I watched her turn and walk away across the parking lot, toward the two-story complex. I had seen the blood again that stained the front of her dress, the now badly puffed cheek, blotches of dark on her fair face, and the swollen, split lower lip jutting hopelessly out in the most poignant image of all of the harm done to her. This is absurd, I was thinking. Do something.

But there was nothing I could find to do. *He* was all around, *he* was everywhere. *He* was a fate she had to absolve by herself. I felt utterly superfluous in the face of this destiny she was taking with her in that white bedraggled dress, adorned with a skewed little crown of diamonds on her head, across that dark asphalt parking lot toward a door somewhere.

I jumped from the cab, my shin stabbing with pain so I almost lost my balance. I held on to the car door. "You *are* perfect, you know that?" I shouted. But she never turned, she kept walking, through an entryway, and was gone.

Dolores

She used to talk us to death at the Westheimer One stand. You could always count on her being out of her cab talking to any other driver who had the misfortune of sharing the stand with her, in a loud voice leaning her big body into his window, into his face. And if there were several cabs, woe to them all, she just went right down the line, each driver in turn forced to endure the same scenario, the same story of success boasted down his throat. For with Dolores it was always success, every night without fail. No one made as much money, no one was as good. And she demanded always to see *your* trip sheet, to see how *you* had done, so there could be no doubt when once she delighted herself with the comparison, enjoyed the triumph.

That we never saw *her* trip sheet didn't seem the point, for she could reel off all the parameters of her success as if she were a computer, right up to the precise moment for that evening: fare per mileage, fare per hour, fare per gallons gas consumption, gross fare, net fare, tips (her many pleased customers, just showering her with favor), and long distance charters, she never let us forget those (somehow, if we believed her, she managed a trip to Fort Polk, Louisiana nearly every week, taking desperate soldiers, desperately late off leave, without even time to wait for a bus apparently, back to their base across the Sabine for a mere, cool $150 charge), etc., etc.

Neither did it matter that her cab might be front of the line and she several vehicles back, boasting at some poor soul's window. If dispatch called the lead cab on the stand she just reached her sizeable bulk right into your vehicle for your mike, didn't even ask you. Once she pressed her huge boobs so hard into my face reaching in for my mike, I thought I would suffocate on that great right breast of hers jammed against my mouth. She remained like that through the entire exchange with dispatch, so I was forced to suck hard for air against the tough fabric of her bra under the knit of her blouse rasping on my teeth and over the entire surface of my tongue. When she pulled away I gasped and nearly fainted.

Yes, she was big. She belonged in a Fellini film with her dimensions. And such *audace* to squash them into you.

Yet, what can I say, we tolerated her, in better moods we even humored her, though most times we just endured her. For in reality we were sorry for her. The greatest driver Yellow Cab ever had or not, real or charlatan, we excused her as best we could. She was far too big, and not just in the bust, to be attractive, and she showed it off by wearing everything tight; even pants, she always wore pants. Any man who might in some strange fit fall for her monstrous bosom, or maybe just out of curiosity want to try her out, would, we were sure, be swallowed. Black Widow death. Without a trace, gone.

But it was not just a joke. And Fellini would have seen

this too, for there was something demonic, febrile in her. It was not just that her face had the hard cast of a man's, but there was trial written into the fibers of that countenance, and those eyes that blazed triumph, a raw red deep within the whites of those eyes that stopped you with an abiding sense of something caged and titanic in all that bigness. Trapped and wanting to be free, like those mighty breasts trapped, and unnaturally it seemed, within the tight, tight blouses she wore, pent-up and caged by her clothes as if they actually wanted to burst right into your face if they could, along with everything else that wanted freedom in that body, or *from* that body, to break right out and seize you.

Yes, I often stared at those breasts, it's true, and not only because they once nearly suffocated me, and I was wary of a repeat. For doing so, just dreaming on them, would help against the insistence and intimidation of her talk, talk, talk when she came to my cab. I would let myself think good thoughts, drift to the fantasy of what wonderful reserves of life were just waiting, and being wasted, in those impressive mammae. I would even marvel sometimes, if caught in the right mood. Truly, she could have been wet nurse to a dozen babies at the same time, there was no doubt.

She could even have been a mother, if there was more doubt. For in the end I could only conclude woe for any child of her womb; forced to suckle on what surely were massive tits burrowing in that bra, to be rammed probably right down the poor child's throat as if it were success itself she was pumping into the tiny body, to go out and conquer as she had, to be Romulus and found Rome. Remus, of course, wouldn't stand a chance.

Okay, maybe I was carried away when my fantasies got to the mother part. But it always seemed my best intentions to romanticize Dolores as she talked and badgered me to death would deteriorate rapidly, unless I could save something by conjuring up what were *my* terms of success for the She-Wolf we saw her as: Motherhood, the Goddess, breasts and chalices forever pouring life into a tired world.

For the world *was* tired, and needed to suck a million cups dry just to function, yet she was competing with us who had made it so. And what did any of us really know about her, anyway, at the heart of that swagger of hers, where likely she was famished, and could only find sustenance by pushing the rest of us back and racing ahead for the Promised Land of success, of milk and honey enough to nourish her? Able to proclaim at least, looking back at us from the finish line, I AM, BECAUSE I AM BEST.

She did that, and we didn't like it. Here she was, the only woman among us on the night shift. Surrounded by men; bigger than any of us for sure, and better (if only for acting it), but surrounded.

What could that have meant for her?

For suddenly, you see, she was gone. And it was like a vacuum at the cab stand. For several nights, finally a week running, she was gone. Then the rumors began, as if to fill that vacuum with something urgently needed, for relief, for a sense to it all, that otherwise her sudden absence made impossibly incoherent and crazy for definition. The story was like a fever of its own at Westheimer One: how she had driven for an independent owner of yellow cabs, not the company fleet as most of us did, and the owner, maybe himself tired of all the talk, maybe tired of feeling a Black Widow male when confronted with her, had decided to take fate into his own hands, make her heel by forcing her to bed with him. Whatever really happened was not clear, and he, whoever he was, remained a shadow, but we learned he had fired her, and was getting word out to the grapevine that she was a manhater a mile deep, with only a penchant for girls in her bed, balling a regular succession of them in her place, wherever that was, being the man she hated to their passive, frightened submission.

I don't even repeat the full length of it, but it was cruel stuff and I wished it would stop. That she could be back among us. At least by her sheer presence to have her say in defense of herself. For I was sure no one would dare bring it up, if she could just return, resume her role as the very best driver among us, at least the champion of bluff, if that's all it was. I granted her that right.

For wasn't that what we as males were supposed to be, if we could carry it off? Whether bluff or reality? Romulus founding Rome, every single one of us? Even if Sabines got raped along the way?

Well, it all finally died down. Dolores became history. Then one Saturday night I got a call from Westheimer One for a pick-up over on Roseland. It was a dreary residential street, of old, dark-brick apartment buildings in square, two-story sameness one after another, and the address given me was right at the dead end, where the street had been cut off by the Southwest Freeway, a dark, unlit corner in the night which required I get out of the cab with a flashlight to confirm the address on the building.

Who else but Dolores answered the door at the top of the landing. She looked tired and cross, and as I greeted her she just walked briskly and coldly by me and down the stairs. I followed her out, and she let herself into the front seat. When I slipped in behind the wheel all I got from her was a curt statement of her destination, another one of these same apartment buildings up toward Westheimer.

"How have you been?" I asked rather timidly, as I eased the meter flag over. "We've missed you at the cab stand."

"Shit you have," she said. I swung the cab around, feeling from her bulk a radiation of rage that silenced anything else I might venture to say. We proceeded up the street. She just stared ahead, her jaw jutting out in defiance from her face, her body inclined forward in her seat. As always she wore pants, and a large woman's purse in her lap didn't add an iota of femininity to the impression she made of almost brutal confrontive tension with the world.

And when we reached her destination, and she asked me to wait, the atmosphere only deteriorated further when she shortly returned and told me to drive to another address in a blunt, vituperative tone that had me increasingly nervous and edgy.

It was Saturday night, a busy time, and dispatch was calling out trips nonstop. Suddenly Dolores yelled, "Why don't you shut up," at the radio, and reached over and clicked it off. At the second address the same thing happened. She asked me to wait, but returned shortly, muttering as she got in, "Damnit, not at home either. She'd said she'd be here." A pause, then she blurted out savagely a third address, as if it were a place she was going to attack.

It went on for an hour like this. Any wish I had to find out the real story of what had happened to end her cab driving was thwarted by my fear of aggravating her further, so I just drove, from one address to the other, the meter, and her rage, adding up.

I don't remember how many places we stopped, all of them apartment buildings around the Montrose district. We even went back to the first two addresses one more time.

She was exhaling harder and harder against the feelings inside her, forcing the air out of her in sudden, breathy thrusts from her large bosom mounting with frustration, bitterness, and what would have seemed natural in any other person to be a long overdue, pent-up need to cry. But she remained dry-eyed, jaw jutting, breathing fiercely just to breathe at all.

After one last failure to find anyone at home, or at least answering the door, she told me to take her back to her place. Ending the string of failures actually seemed to help. She relaxed a little, into a coldness that was still incommunicative. "Well, we've missed you, Dolores, and I wish you well in the future," I said as I stopped in front of her apartment at the dead end of Roseland. She said nothing, but got out of the cab and walked away. I jumped out. "Dolores, hey, what about the fare?" I shouted.

"Fuck the fare," was all I heard, as she disappeared through the front door of the building.

I debated running in there and demanding my fare. After an hour it was not inconsiderable. I thought of calling dispatch and getting the police over here. They willingly helped us out in situations like this. But it all seemed suddenly rather pointless and stupid. She had her problems, after all. I decided to pay the meter out of my own pocket. It being Saturday night, maybe I could make it up. I turned the radio back on and drove away.

But the night would test me. It grew slack, unusually so, and over the next four hours, up to the 2 AM closing of the bars, I managed only a few short trips. My anger at Dolores waxed and waned, my sense of insult. More than once I was heavily tempted to go back there and demand my payment.

But I never did. I kept telling myself she had her problems, and maybe they required some sacrifice.

It was two nights later. I was out in another sector of the city when, as it was reported, Dolores suddenly appeared with her purse walking up to the Westheimer One cab stand. Several cabs were parked there, and the drivers all recognized her. But she gave no one time even to call out her name, instead slipping immediately into the front seat of the lead car. He was a relatively new driver, an immigrant from Yugoslavia who had gained a reputation for friendliness. I did not know him very well, but he certainly knew Dolores from his first days on the job, well enough at least to greet her amicably by name and ask her where she wanted to go. She told him to hand over his cab. Thinking maybe he misunderstood her he asked again in his friendly way where she wanted to go. She said again she wanted his cab, and to get out. At this he apparently laughed nervously (the driver behind remembered him laughing in an odd way and saying, "No, you don't mean it, of course"). In reply she pulled from her big purse a pistol, and without hesitation emptied the barrel into the young man at the wheel. The report indicated five bullets.

Point blank. He was evidently trying to open the door when she pulled out the pistol, and his head fell backward into the street when the door swung open from the pressure of his shattered body as she unloaded on him, precise, rapid-fire, and loud.

An HPD patrol car was catty-corner on Montrose, parked in front of a bar, and the two officers were just getting back into their vehicle after investigating a scuffle inside the premises. They came running, shouting at the sound of the shots.

Her pistol was empty. Blood poured all over the street from the limp body half in and half out of the cab. She was arrested on the spot.

It was hushed at Westheimer One for a long time after that. More a vacuum than ever.

Sphinx

I told myself I should have gone to Rothko's Chapel and stared at those black canvases. Something was wrong, and it needed at least a face. Maybe those black canvases...

The heat was insufferable, but that was just it: it seemed more than a reading of Fahrenheit, but a statement. As ineffable as those black canvases, and as foreboding. Something in it made the soul boil.

It was late in the day, the dead of summer, and I was answering a call to a large apartment complex far to the southwest. Out here the city's edge seemed to slam into the white sky and the fierce juggernaut of the low sun over the coastal plains. The waves of heat radiating couldn't have been greater if the horizon had been a rim of braze soldering shut the sky in a lock-tight, hermetic lid—like a grand, diabolic Astrodome the sun had engineered for itself over the great sprawl of Houston, expressly to come indoors—The Great Indoors of Houston.

But in the joke there seemed a hint of truth this evening, a judgment. *Those black canvases were painted for the sun, yet hung in the confinement of a room.*

I approached my destination, fighting off the sun that

was dead ahead in my windshield, and wrapped in a viscous package of heat that seemed to emanate as much from inside me as from out. I kept looking south, but no cloud bank rolling up, promising rain. No southerly, brine-laden winds. The Gulf withheld its plenty from us. I pulled into the parking lot beside the complex and waited momentarily in case my passenger came out. The sun burned the side of my face, sweat sloshed under my shirt; and I thought of rain. I wanted water, lots of it, one of those gargantuan downpours that were just a matter of time this season, sky-fest of cold, roaring flood, when slabs of water cascaded the windshield and swamped the impotent thrash of wipers, the metal skin of the car thundered like kettledrums, the storm sewers of Houston filled in minutes and every street turned river and rampage. When all you could do was find a high place, in this flat city ramming your car above the curb was the best you could do, parking on the sidewalk or someone's lawn to wait. And up the water came anyway, isolating houses into islands, shoving at the car and pushing in at the door, already slapping the hot engine hissing, rising above the baseboard as you scrambled up your seat, coming higher and higher yet, black, rising, and would it stop, would it stop, would it stop . . . ?

And people sometimes drowned, misjudging the dip of the road beneath a railway overpass, probably frantic to get home, determined to get through. But the depth would prove astonishing, suck the car right down, swamping the engine dead and filling the interior cold and imperturbably, already to the roof outside. They couldn't push their door open against the pressure, if their windows were electrical they couldn't roll them down. Their screams hopeless in the rising, heartless and huge, of water, up the final inches of space they claw for to breathe, finally crushing out their panic in that ultimate, horrible simplicity of cold, bold water.

Perverse maybe to want this. *But then there were those paintings of Rothko. I couldn't get them off my mind. Flood of a dark, desperate soul, that took you under and deep.* Perverse. I didn't deny it. But then there was this Houston heat, that could make you feel you were breathing beneath water anyway, but hot, under the hot, cloying torpor of it drowning anyway. It all seemed judgment suddenly, as I fought hard to breathe, it seemed truth, operating from the poles of extremes that formed the only possible flexion of reality in a climate of extremes that was Houston this time of year (and hurricane season coming). What else to think of a city that doubled in size every few years because of a total, extreme dependency on air-conditioning and climate control and machine for its very existence in these wide open, dangerous spaces it could not possibly survive as the infra-structure and superstructure and psyche it was, except behind reinforced walls and in the machine-produced currents of cold, artificial air.

It even made me refuse to use the air-con between trips, pretend to tolerate the heat. How, I wondered, had the Kar-ankawa Indians managed it in this place, before the white man and progress invaded their world and wiped them out? Tall and stately, their naked bodies smeared in stink of alliga-tor grease to keep off the mosquitoes, they must have been a stillness, an acceptance, suffering simply the fierce heat and sudden floods, the tornadoes and hurricanes, the disease of

173

the marsh flats and bayous—they must have been a dignity. In them the buoyancy of natural man maybe, who knew he was profoundly contingent to be alive at all, that the powers which allowed him life were well outside his compass, and always would be. Or else they stood in judgment.

But not us. No, we were in a rush. Modern, fast, air-conditioned, and insular. As I had been in a rush to get here. And someone inside was in a rush to get somewhere else, though they weren't coming out to meet me. Enough waiting. I got out of the cab, forcing deep breaths against the heat, feeling fierce and thoroughly out of sorts. I didn't fit in in any way, that was for sure. I wasn't modern man, or natural man. Just a fool of a cab driver, I guess. I tramped across the parking lot, heavy with perspiration and some vague sense of demise.

I finally found the apartment, along a hallway inside one of the buildings. I rang the doorbell, and waited a while before the door opened: a girl, maybe eighteen, with cropped blond hair, tiny features, standing diminutive in front of me, looking rather like a boy despite her leather miniskirt and black heels. She wore no make-up, and stared at my chest, not my eyes, as if she were in a trance. "Cab," I said. "There was a call." She said nothing, but turned mechanically and went back into her apartment. She reappeared a moment later with a small purse, closed and locked the door, and without a word proceeded down the hall. She was clumsy in her heels, as if they were too big, wobbling in them a little, and suddenly I noticed her head jerk sideways in a strange way. I caught up with her, and led her out to the cab. I opened the door to the back seat opposite the driver's side and let her in, but before I could shut it she grabbed the door handle and forcefully pulled the door from my grasp and slammed it.

I slipped behind the wheel. "And where you going to?" I asked, holding irritation in while looking back at her over the seat. She was pressed against her door and had begun to fidget, as if she itched all over, jerking her head sideways and back in a manner patently bizarre, her eyes narrowed and glassy. She had a tiny mouth that was opened into an O, she was small-breasted and petite beneath a lemon-colored blouse, and her movements were abrupt and toy-like.

"Are you all right?" I asked.

"Why aren't we going?" she suddenly shouted, her blue eyes blazing fierce at me.

"Because I don't know where you want to go. I just asked you your destination."

"I told you already. Can't you hear?" Her head popped violently sideways toward her window.

"Are you all right?" I asked again. If she had had insects inside her clothes I don't think she could have been more jumpy.

"Shit, why aren't we going?"

"But *where* are we going?" I said in exasperation, and then just sighed. "Okay, I didn't hear you the first time." And she abruptly shouted name and address of a nightclub over in the vicinity of Sharpstown Mall. "That's all I needed. Thank you." I pushed the meter flag over and pulled away.

I remembered seeing the club before, and that TOPLESS in bright neon swam all over the exterior. I looked at the reflection of the girl in my mirror. Eighteen, certainly no older. "Do you work as a waitress?" I asked, unable to stay quiet as she fidgeted and jumped in the back seat.

"What?" she said loudly.

"Do you work as a waitress?"

"Are you stupid or something? What else would I be doing there?"

"Just thought I'd ask." I was making my way east, the low sunlight shining up from the swaths of yellow grass and scrub separating the new housing tracts and office buildings and apartments out here where development was still underway.

"Don't you have air-conditioning?" she barked at me. "I'm burning up back here."

"Oh, of course, of course. I'm sorry." I turned it on max, then rolled up my window and, leaning over while driving, the one opposite. "I apologize," I reiterated, feeling the cold, blowing, mechanical air on my face as a stark and unappeasing relief from the heat in the sudden insularity of the cab, heightened almost to claustrophobia for me by the presence of this passenger. But I realized she had me severely off-balance to have forgotten the air-con with a fare aboard. "I guess I just like it hot," I said, in lame excuse for my lapse.

"They keep it cold where I work. I get goosebumps, and then the men want to touch me."

"Do they touch you? Is that allowed?"

"God, are you stupid. What do you think?" Her body continued to jerk in odd ways as she spoke. The glare of the sun in my mirror made it hard to see her reflection, but the silhouette of her head kept jumping into the glass this way and that in a strange, heartless shadow play that distracted me constantly from the road. "And their hands are cold," she added with a shudder in her voice. "Cold, cold."

I turned the air-con down a couple of notches on the fan control, thinking maybe she was getting cold now. Not wanting, maybe, to be confused with the men awaiting her in that place.

"Doesn't the bouncer protect you from the customers?" I asked.

"Shit, he's the worst. He tried to fuck me after hours last night." She jumped suddenly, like someone had pinched her. "They're all over me in that place, because I'm small. The other girls are big. You know, boobs you can get your hands on. But they don't touch them, they touch me. 'Little Tits,' that's what they call me in there."

I wanted to ask her why she worked there, but it instantly seemed a stupid, pointless question, and died on my tongue. Suddenly she gave out a strange yelp, half a little dog and half the meow of a cat, her body lifting from the seat as if in horror of some ugly thing that had landed beside her.

"Are you all right?"

"Fuckin' A, mister. Now just drive, why don't you." And she emitted another one of those hapless yelps, flinging her back against the door and raising her arms against something grotesque. The sun suddenly hit my mirror dead on, exploding my eyes in a flash that sent me reeling back to the street and just driving, driving to get this girl to where she was going. I welcomed a left in the direction of Sharpstown, and freedom from that harsh sun in my mirror. But she came into fuller view now in the brilliance of the horizontal sun irradiating the side of her face. Her pale skin went fiercely auburn, her blond hair ginger and strange, like fire was lit within it.

She was fire, and shuddering from cold back there.

"Do you still want the air-conditioning?" I asked. "Tell me if you're cold, I'll turn it down or off."

She bounced forward, her head suddenly right beside mine, her arms draped over the front seat. "No, mister, keep it on, and higher. I'm burning up back here, I told you. Don't you hear anything?"

I turned it up to high fan again, directing the flow at her face. She was so close her reflection filled my mirror—her eyes, blue and nervous, were framed in the rectangle of the glass like a mask with a life of its own, almost staring right back at me, but not quite, eerily missing. She gazed instead right by the mirror, down the road to what awaited her. Her short strands of hair danced from her head in the cold blast of the air-con fanning around her, a flickering, feral presence at each edge of that mask. We entered shadow now, closed in by buildings, the sun horizon-level and sinking behind them. No longer lit up like fire, she seemed more and more a creature of the cold air rushing at her, her face freezing to a marble stillness beside my shoulder, the way she gripped the front seat with her arms now muting the tension and twitchings of her body, her eyes beginning to sink inward, wide and without focus. She became finally a trance, thoroughly rigid. Her hair alone had any life, bouncing like a boy's cut in the cold air that seemed to have seized thoroughly her soul.

Then suddenly I saw that mask staring right at me. Her eyes had found me in the mirror. It made my skin creep.

Thoroughly cold, thoroughly judgment. Her wide eyes as foreboding as a statue seemed to see right to the heart of something terrible I was. I couldn't have been more horrified than if I had met the Sphinx outside the walls of Thebes. But whatever riddle was in those eyes I couldn't answer. I doubled my speed and kept my own eyes to the road, but checking again I saw she was still there, still staring dead in my face.

Moments later I watched her walk, in those haphazard heels of hers, toward the door of the club. She held her arms straight and away from her body, dangling her purse like a child would a small tote bag. She approached with a certain caution, through the host of cars already parked in front. Suddenly I saw her head jerk sideways the way it had before.

The few thin clouds flared out in corals and pinks overhead. TOPLESS blared out in bright neon against the dying wash of color in the west, the building itself dark and angular in silhouette. She opened the door and looked a moment inside before entering. Then she was gone, into the cold. A big arm reached out and closed the door shut.

The air-con off and windows down I felt the heat roll in on me. But it did no good. Goosebumps jumped all over my skin, I shivered. She had laid a freeze on me, a judgment. The Sphinx.

All night long I was on the run, from judgment, for rain, running. Wanting only black, black to rid me of her face. But it did no good. Those eyes were frozen in my mirror, grafted on my soul.

In the myth everyone but Oedipus was eaten, and he later stabbed his eyes out.

Postscript: Rothko's Chapel

Black is the night of this city I've lived. And black are these canvases. Rothko's silence in paint, black paint.

I quit this morning, returning to the cab lot, unable to escape her eyes in my mirror. Sphinx. The judgment of a girl. The judgment of six months behind the wheel of 621. Unable to escape.

And came to this chapel, lit only by the sun through the skylight above. Where redemption is only the sun upon the black of these canvases, setting them in motion, giving them life.

Eyes. Her eyes, and all of them, thousands peering back at me from within the mobile hint of presence, presence in absence, of these paintings—the bodies, the eyes, roaming these textured surfaces of black, a restless, eerie horde. Bound by these frames, but terrible how they stare and push, press against absence. Terrible their beauty.

I knew them. Where are they now? I knew them, night after night. But what are they now? Presence in absence. Here, because the sun through the skylight sets them in motion, is their life.

And among all those eyes, that stare, move imperceptibly, restless in the tension of their absence—the black that is all of them—are two: *my* eyes.

Do they see a future? Is there a future?

These tales are only a past. Absence. In that alone is presence. In that alone is hope.

Outside, the sun is rising. . .

CPSIA information can be obtained at www.ICGtesting.com
Printed in the USA
LVOW132300230412

278838LV00002B/1/P